Man 'Most Grown

D1556873

Marilyn Bishop Sha

[handwritten inscription: To dear Cindy and Tom — Solomon's story continues! Hope you enjoy — Thanks for many years of wonderful friendship. Love, Marilyn]

This book is dedicated to all the intrepid settlers who tamed early Florida, particularly the Bishops, who settled in Jefferson County in the early 1830s, and the Shaws, who settled in Alachua County in @1866. Along with the Native Americans, they set the standard as true Floridians.

Man 'Most Grown

Copyright @2016 by Marilyn Bishop Shaw This title is also available as a Kindle ebook

Cover Art: Annette Toy Shaw

Cover Design: Jason Taylor

Library of Congress Catalog in Publication Data
Shaw, Marilyn Bishop
Man 'Most Grown/Marilyn Bishop Shaw ISBN: 1530978262
ISBN-13: 978-1530978267
Historical Fiction/Florida History/ Reconstruction/Homesteading/ Pioneering/Coming of Age

CHAPTER ONE

June 1870 – It was so hot a body could see the heat rise from the broiling earth. The tall, lean young man chopped steadily, rhythmically, dollops of sweat flying from his body with every arc of the axe. He reached for a bandana, dipped it in the nearby water bucket, and leaned on the axe wearily. The water wasn't nearly cool, but just wetting his face was some relief. *Not much,* Solomon thought, *but better than nothing.* Before it could evaporate the beads of water would be joined by sweat until there was no difference between the salty and fresh droplets.

Solomon Freeman spoke out loud. "Lord, I know I ain't seen many summers yet, but this got to be the hottest one ever in my life and it only June." He interrupted his conversation with the Lord for a slurp from the water dipper then continued. "I hate to think what it be in August. A body could pure explode into fire." One more splash of water, a quick shake, a deep breath, and the boy began chopping all over again.

Aim for the windshake. Whap! *That's it; that hardwood split right in half neat as you please, just like Papa said it would.* With every heavy stroke, Solomon fell deeper into a reverie of the past. It felt like more than four years since the Freemans began establishing their place in freedom. In just under a year they would claim their land patent and own eighty whole acres free and clear. *If we can hang on long enough to survive and, Lord, times I got some doubts on that.*

Solomon glanced across the yard to the clothesline and smiled. He knew his mother wouldn't take long to haul in the bed clothes. She wouldn't get out of earshot from the house ever. She was hardly strong enough yet to do laundry but that little woman wasn't about to let others carry her weight. A smile crossed the boy's face as he pictured his baby sister sleeping peacefully in the crib that Manuel and the other drovers made for her. What a surprise Sarah had been – even more, what a miracle.

As he sucked in a breath to hoist the axe again, Solomon smelled smoke – faint, but definitely smoke. Before he could call warning, Lela's head whipped toward the house as she dropped the sheet in her hand. "Noooo!" she screamed as she raced into the house.

As he cornered the house, a tiny wisp of smoke escaping from the back of the chimney told him all he needed to know. "Mama!" he yelled. "Sarah!"

Lela tried to douse the fire, but made little progress. Solomon pulled her away from the fireplace. "Mama, get Sarah out of here. Grab what you can and get out of here!"

Following Solomon's commands seemed natural as Lela had become used to her almost fifteen-year-old son taking charge better than most grown men. She stumbled to her bedroom, scooping up three-month-old Sarah, a picture from the wall, and the few clothes hanging on the wall.

By the time Lela deposited her first load far enough from the house for safety and returned to the house Solomon was snatching their precious collection of books and tossing them into Sarah's crib. When the crib was full, he hauled it outside, too. "Mama, get back," he ordered. "I'll get what I can."

The mud fireplace was in full blaze and she couldn't return to her bedroom, but she could reach one side of their stores. "Oh, Lord, we can't lose all our food, we just can't," she moaned as she and Solomon rescued a few bags of meal and flour, a bolt of fabric, and a few cans of milk before the fire got too hot.

Gulping fresh air as he turned back toward the house, Solomon spat orders to his mother. "Move this stuff away and see to Sarah. You listen to me this time and stay out!" Before she reached to stop him, he was inside the smoking cabin again. Turning to follow his instructions, Lela saw Moses hanging on to Sally as they raced in from the corn field. He arrived in time to move their salvaged goods farther from the incinerating house while she settled a howling Sarah.

Then Lela dipped and Moses ran to throw buckets of water on the near side of the bunk house. "Can't let this go, Lela," the man yelled. "Got to save it!"

Solomon tore blindly through the curtain of black, stinking pine tar smoke back to the supplies. He dropped and crawled toward the side that wasn't yet aflame. Finding a piece of oilcloth, he raked whatever he could onto the square, grabbed up the corners, and stumbled toward the door again.

He fell through the door into the yard and his father was there with a wet rag. "Papa," the boy wheezed, "take this. I'm going one more time."   Moses hadn't gotten a word out before Solomon had tied the wet rag around his face and pushed back into the tiny cabin. The house, little more than a lean-to, might not have seemed much, but it was all they had. And it was theirs. Solomon's cot was farther from the fireplace than anything in the blazing structure. He scooped his clothes from the wall, pulled a metal box from under the bed, three books from a little shelf, and wrapped it all in his extra shirt, tossing the bundle over his shoulder.

He moved into his doorway and stopped. The place was so smoky he couldn't see a thing, but he knew exactly where to reach. He hung the coiled whip around his neck, staggered toward the front door, and paused again. This time he blindly reached over the doorway and grabbed the searing shotgun with his free right hand. It would have been better if he'd grabbed the wooden stock but he wrapped his hand around the gun in the first place he touched -- just above the barrel break.

His father, just short of panic, awaited the stumbling figure leaving the cabin. "You ain't goin' back in there, son. Don't even think on it." Solomon's lungs burned as he fell to his knees.

"Take this, Papa," he rasped as his father dragged him further from the flames, "I'll come when I catch my breath." That's when Solomon went limp and fell face down in the sandy yard. Through gray unconsciousness Solomon saw familiar images.

He saw a little family risking life and limb to make a farm out of the unclaimed North Florida wilds. Isolation had worked for them. A few – very few – friendly people had stumbled across them and a few decidedly unfriendly ones had turned up, too.

He struggled to breathe through unconsciousness, reliving the fight against the weather in every extreme imaginable – and some unimaginable. Solomon shivered as his mind saw the horrible ice storm in the spring of '68. Surely, that was the worst. Or maybe the hurricane was worse. He could feel the storm-sharpened rain drops. Either one could take the prize as long as neither happened again.

He felt the physical exhaustion from planting, tending, and harvesting every acre they could clear, building what they could and patching and mending harnesses and tools long after they had served their usefulness. And he sensed the added fatigue of a boy too young doing a man's work.

Though he couldn't know it, Solomon's parents had dragged him under an oak tree and were applying cooling cloths to his face. Moses and Lela couldn't know why his tense, tossing body suddenly relaxed.

Locked inside his unmoving body, Solomon felt the freedom of woods rambles and saw a circus prancing around him of the fish and game he brought to the table that kept them from starving. Despite the lean times and the scary ones, never had Solomon questioned leaving Hill's Run in Georgia. As clearly as a spring sky he saw the lean-to they built just in time for the first winter as it mysteriously took improved forms.

It seemed like he had relived those distant images in an instant and, as he opened his eyes, he saw that their home was gone. His scorched hands were wrapped and he felt a cool cloth bathing his smutty face. To Moses and Lela it seemed like an age that their boy had been unconscious.

As they settled into their makeshift beds in the bunkhouse that night Moses worried, "Don't know we had a choice, but sure hope Pete Harker don't mind us putting in here like this."

"Be ashamed to even think that, Moses Freeman," Lela scolded gently. Before her husband could speak she continued. "Yes, this bunk house does belong to Pete, but it's on our place and here with our cooperation."

"Mama's right, Papa," Solomon interjected through a raspy cough. "Ain't nobody woulda helped us pull ourselves into this bunk house any quicker than Pete and you know it. Was he here, he'd 'bout be mad to hear you talk such." Solomon tried to take a deep breath and dissolved into coughs again.

Her son's smoky cough abated and Lela had the last word. "Now – the afternoon rain doused the fire, we're safe – except for the scratchy throat and burns on Solomon's hands and I think they'll heal up in good time. We have shelter, we have enough we won't go hungry, and our little Sarah is slumbering peacefully. There'll be nothing more tonight but a good night's sleep before your yammering wakes her." That ended all discussion and the breathing of exhausted sleep filled the room, disturbed only by occasional weak coughs.

It took a full week after the fire to work back into a routine. Solomon's burns and singes were healing well except for the still raspy throat and the palm of his right hand which received the worst damage from the scorching shotgun. He felt badly that he couldn't work at full strength, but somehow the essential chores were done. Two half-strength men couldn't run a farm and nothing extra was accomplished, but animals and crops couldn't be put off if they were expected to feed a family.

Between tending Sarah and scratching together two meager meals a day, Lela foraged through the sticky, stinky char of the only home they had ever owned. After hours of work, all she dug out was a few metal plates and the metal parts of kitchen tools. Her biggest relief was finding her treasured cast iron cook pot and Dutch oven.

If the rain hadn't come when it did, things would have been even worse. Nearly every night they tried to brighten their spirits by reminding themselves that if the fire had reached the dry underbrush in the nearby woods, they could have lost the bunkhouse, barns and pens, animals and all. It could have blown for miles before burning out. That these were facts, for which they were thankful, didn't lessen their exhaustion and anguish.

About two weeks after the fire Lela carefully inspected Solomon's burns after he had washed up for supper. She took special note of his right hand. "I don't like the way this looks, Moses. What do you think?"

"Most don't look bad, Lela. Your doctoring got it just about healt."

"May be but my doctoring hasn't done much for this spot." She pointed at a raised round of scarlet flesh with an unknown but distinct shape marked by graying ridges. Beyond that, was the telltale white of infection. "I used my burn leaves, Moses, just like always. Most times that just soothes and heals in a few days . . ." Her voice faded.

"I couldn't see what I was grabbing, Mama. Just knew we needed the gun -- out -- of -- the house." Solomon still wheezed when he exerted himself or talked too much, unable to get a full chest of air.

Moses strode quickly away from the cook fire then returned with the shotgun, inspecting the metal shaft around the trigger as he walked. "Look here." He held out the gun and pointed to a round insignia that looked like a swirl. "Ain't that it? Ain't that what on Solomon's hand?"

"You right, Papa. Now why you reckon they put a fancy thing like that on a gun?" Solomon inquired.

"I'm not really worried about why it's there," Lela proclaimed impatiently as she looked more closely at the heel of the boy's hand. Leaning in to smell it she added, "I'm more worried about what this hand looks like right now."

"Oh, Mama," Solomon said. "I just been using it too much. I'll try to be extra careful to use it less a few days and you'll see it get better fast."

"We seen burns like this." Moses' face turned stoney. "You ain't seen it, boy, but your Mama and me has. All along she get dabs of special 'coction from the big house. Good batch of clean lard worked on lashes but that mix was 'bout only thing worked 'tall on such as this. Many a night she sneak into barn to a chained runner and doctor him."

"What did they have if it wasn't lashes, Papa?" Solomon had come appreciate his father's initial distress toward his weapon and tool of choice – a sixteen foot whip.

But Moses was finally convinced that Pete Harker, who introduced whips to the boy, had taught Solomon proper use and restraint. He hadn't wanted his son to have anything to do with the very object that caused so much anguish among his people.

Glad his son was inexperienced enough not to know, Moses was also aware that there was much about slave life that he needed to understand or he would never know the value of the freedom they now enjoyed. Lela had hoped Solomon would never know the ugliest parts of their former lives. Her glance toward Moses indicated that she, too, knew it was time Solomon learned more about their history.

Moses looked hard into his son's eyes. "Runner get caught he get taught lessons. Get whupped fifty lashes, marked with cut off ear, or . . . ," Moses paused with emotion then forced the words out. "Or he be branded."

"Papa?" Solomon shuddered, watching his father walk away. "You ain't . . ."

"No son," Lela answered for her husband. "He saw his papa branded. He was just a little boy and already showing signs of fight so the master made little Moses watch as the overseer used the very same brand his papa used on the cows. The master thought it would teach Moses a lesson."

"Mister Walker did that?"

Moses had wandered away from them and Lela continued quietly. "Oh, no. Moses wasn't always at Hill's Run. He owned us right enough, there's no way to pretend he didn't, but Mister Walker didn't do such things."

"What was the brand like? Where was it?"

"Moses doesn't speak of it much but he said it was a graceful curving design at the top of his daddy's arm so it was easy to spot. The one on your hand must remind him of it."

Solomon barely touched the mark on his hand and shook his head slowly. "So much I don't know, Mama. So much I don't know."

"Yes, son, there were terrible things. We tried to protect you from the worst and were lucky to be at Hill's Run – luckier even than the others there," Lela said sadly. "Maybe that was a mistake. Maybe you need to at least hear the worst parts so you never lose sight of the past."

Shaking off the gloom Lela announced firmly. "Don't lose sight of your future, either, young man. Tomorrow you take that hand of yours to the doctor."

The rest of the season was spent dodging summer rain storms and slapping mosquitoes as the field corn and kitchen garden were brought in. Moses drew into himself and the man child toiled even harder to make up for their losses.

On a sultry August afternoon Moses brought Sally back to the mule lot and noticed Lela sitting under the oak tree. He watched as Sarah fretted on a pallet at her mother's feet while Lela shucked a few ears of fresh field corn.

Moses leaned silently against the wall and watched her work with admiration. Carefully, she cut the kernels from the cob into an old enamel bowl. Then, with the blade of a sharp little knife she scraped the cob, its milk dripping into another bowl.

Moses was puzzled. If Lela planned corn for supper there would be more corn and she'd have taken it to the bunk house to prepare. And he'd never seen her separate the kernels from the scraping. When the last cob was tossed toward the mule lot she poured some of the corn milk into something Moses recognized, an oil cloth cone Lela fashioned with a little opening at its narrow end. The realization hit him physically as he dropped his head and felt tears well up in his eyes. He couldn't watch any more.

"Lela," he said softly so he wouldn't startle her or Sarah, "how long you been doin' this?"

"Moses!" she replied with a start. She looked down at her task and asked, "How long have you been there?"

"Plenty long enough to see you keepin' things from me. How long you been doin' this?" he asked insistently.

"Just a few days, Moses. I added a little water to the last of the canned milk, but it's gone and I thought we could get by on this for a while." Her gaunt face exposed her exhaustion. It also exposed her guilt and inadequacy. "I can't even feed my child, Moses."

Her husband kneeled at her side and held her as she wept. "Don't you fret yourself over this. Ain't no baby anyplace ask for no better mama. Lots more to it than milk." Lifting her chin, his eyes bored through to her soul. "Now you hear me, Lela Freeman. We ain't had much and we been hit hard losing what we did have. But we been hit hard afore and we got through." She blinked her relief. "You think on what we had when we come here, girl. A wagon, a few tools and supplies, and us. We a sight better than that now I say."

Her quivering lips whispered, "I know, Moses. I just wish . . ."

"And you just quit your wishin'. First light tomorrow Solomon gon' take you and Sarah to New Troy. We ain't so bad off we caint feed our little girl proper. You git everything you need to see to her right. You git what it take to set you right, too. You know you got run down."

The big man's face was soft and stern all at once and he lifted his wife's chin. "And you hear this, Lela. You never been one to keep secrets from me and I won't have you startin' it now. Not to ease my feelin's, not for nothin', do you hear?"

Lela drew in a long, slow breath and stared directly into Moses' eyes to speak her pledge.

"You just made a promise, girl, and I ain't meanin' for you to break it."

"I know, Moses, I know." She leaned into his arms for only an instant before Sarah made her message clear. Lela cradled her and put the corn milk bottle in her child's mouth, thankful that she had a man such as Moses Freeman.

Up and dressed at dawn, even Sarah sensed something special. Going to town – even a little place like New Troy – was an excitement all in itself. The last thing Solomon did before he and Lela boarded the wagon was take two coins from his metal box, just a few coins remaining. He didn't know what had happened yesterday, but knew his Papa meant for him to replace the necessary food, medicine, and household goods that were lost in the fire. He also knew that his real work would come when he had to
make sure his mother truly got everything she needed for the few dollars they had. *Mama come home still scrimpin', Papa be in a fury for sure.*

As they entered the mercantile a new little bell at the top of the door called Mr. Hart from the back room. He began with his usual greeting, "May I help . . ." Then he saw the bundle in Lela's arms. "Why, Mrs. Freeman, what do you have there?"

"A baby, Mr. Hart," Lela laughed, "you've seen a baby before, haven't you?"

"Oh, of course I have. I just haven't seen this baby. Heard about it though. You'd think Granny Ma gave birth herself," Mr. Hart chuckled, mentally noting how thin and wan she was.

Almost as an afterthought Lela looked up at Solomon saying, "Speaking of Granny Ma, you know we'll have to save time to stop by and see her."

"I say so," Mr. Hart laughed. "If she found out you came here without seeing her, she might go right out to your place to tell you about it!" None of them would want Granny Ma's ire. She was a formidable woman of indeterminant age and infinite authority. Mr. Hart refocused on Sarah. "A girl I think?"

"Yessir," Solomon said proudly as Lela unwrapped the blanket. "This is my little sister, Sarah Elizabeth Freeman."

"Well, I never . . ." Mr. Hart couldn't finish his statement for he surely had never. He had never seen a colored infant so close. Like many of his neighbors who still hadn't warmed to the Freemans, he once wouldn't have accepted coloreds into his store at all. Now, here he was being downright friendly. T. R. Hart, never at a loss for words, was speechless.

Gently, he stroked the baby's delicate cheek thinking what a mortal wonder it was that a baby could be so perfectly beautiful. That was another never. Never had he thought to describe a little pickaninny as beautiful. Then again, if he was to tell the truth about it, he would have to say her mother was beautiful, too.

Finally, regaining his composure, he whispered, "Sarah Freeman, after my very own Laura, you are the prettiest little one I ever saw."

When Lela's green eyes met Mr. Hart's he knew she understood his struggle. "Thank you, Mr. Hart. We think she's just about perfect, too."

Mr. Hart's tiny store provided basic household goods, a kitchen knife and big spoon, and staple supplies. Lela hesitantly invested in a length of soft white cotton that could be used for Sarah's swaddling, bandages, shirts – most anything.

A stop at Granny Ma's house earned Lela a jar of tonic and a sermon for letting herself run down so much. She cuddled and cooed to Sarah and presented her with a length of thick, soft cotton cloth which Solomon knew cost her dearly. "Ain't no mama ever had 'nough swaddlin' and know you can't have much after the fire," she huffed, fussing over the baby. "This ain't much but it cut up into some good wraps fer that baby girl." Turning to Lela she added, "An' mebbe it keep you from washin' nasty ones ever' day."

The ride home gave a cheered mother and son uninterrupted time to talk. "I hated to leave your Papa working so hard. I wish he had come. He's just tied himself to that farm more than ever and I worry for him." Lela smiled and looked Heavenward. "I have to admit it was good to have a little break."

"Sure was, Mama, and we had to get supplies."

"I can't believe you bought three of those baby bottles with the nipples on them." Lela continued in disbelief, "And every last can of milk that Mr. Hart had. What made you do such a thing?"

"Never know when we'll get back to the store or what Mr. Hart will have when we do get there," Solomon said matter-of-factly as he smiled down on Sarah's fuzzy head. "And my little sister ain't gon' want for nothin'." His uncompromising voice sounded like his father's, just not quite as deep yet. "My Mama neither," he added mysteriously.

Lela just smiled. *That boy is up to something and I'll know what it is when he's ready for me to. So much like his Papa.*

CHAPTER TWO

Fall, 1870 -- Indian summer had passed and autumn had fallen. "Solomon?" called a voice from the bunkhouse doorway. "Solomon, where are you?"

"What's wrong Mama? What do you need?" the boy sputtered through ragged breaths as he raced toward the front of the bunk house.

Lela said softly, "I didn't mean to alarm you, son. I just wondered where you were."

"I was chopping wood, Mama. It's not cold yet, but we still need wood. Papa always says a body can't have too much wood stacked up."

"Yes, your Papa does say that – a lot!" she chuckled. Concern was all over her face. "Don't you think you've done enough for today, Solomon? Why don't you work on something else and go back to the wood pile tomorrow? Did you realize you've been chopping wood almost constantly since lunch and we only have about an hour or so before sundown?"

A glance upward told him that he'd lost all track of time and his mother was right. "I could stand a break from it." Flexing and massaging his right hand he added, "This hand could use a rest, too, I guess. Anyhow, I didn't know it was so late and the animals have to be put up for the night and fed."

"At least that'll be a change instead of hefting that axe again today." The petite woman inspected the still tender hand. The doctor had treated it when they were in New Troy but it still worried Lela. "I don't like the look of this hand, Solomon. It shouldn't be bothering you so much."

"Oh, it's alright, Mama," he assured her, hating giving her more to worry about. He flexed his painfully stiff hand reflexively. "It's just gripping the axe so long's all." Trying to deflect Lela's concerns Solomon reminded her, "Mama, it left its mark but this hand ain't life and death."

Lela's hand gently touched her son's arm. "I don't know how you do it, Solomon; you just keep on going like your life depends on it."

"Ain't just my life, Mama. Wouldn't be a problem if it was, but it ain't," he said gruffly. "More important things to think on than me." Solomon sounded almost mad though he wasn't really. She walked with her son to the barn to stow the day's harnesses and other tools. *Our lives do depend on it,* she thought. *This boy is not quite fifteen and carries the weight of us all.*

Worry was written all over Lela's face. "Where **is** your papa, son?"

"Feedin' up, Mama. His arm just won't hold out for chopping wood, so he does a lot of the other chores."

"Just don't overdo, Solomon. Besides, slow and steady . . ."

"I know – slow and steady wins the race," Solomon grumbled. *Lord knows, I heard that enough.* As Lela returned to the house, yet again he admired his mother's regal bearing and natural grace. Surely God had made something special in her. Then he stretched his back and finished putting the barn to rights. Knowing his father would feed and gather in the smaller stock, he made sure the mules and Swamp Foot were settled for the day with plenty of water and some corn cobs to chew on.

Seeing that were still a few minutes before sundown, Solomon returned to the woodpile. He finished stacking a cord next to the two already stacked and started a new one with the remaining wood.

Moses soon approached. Always a tall, full-bodied man, his body slumped like old age. Even his voice wasn't as strong as it used to be. "My Lawd, boy, you gon' chop ever' tree in the woods today? It nigh to dark, son."

Glad for another excuse to breathe, Solomon smiled half-heartedly. "Oh, I'm all right, Papa. Only stacking what's left. Just want to get ahead a little."

"Them cords look good, son. Be the savin' of us come winter." Moses meant to encourage his son. He didn't know how dead his voice sounded.

Moses watched Solomon finish with the wood, loathing the idea that he must ask for help. The huge man shifted from foot to foot until Solomon stopped again, a little impatient. "Papa, what's ailin' you?"

"I'm 'bout good as I gon' get, son, but that ain't none too good these days." Moses paused then spoke again, pain and frustration seeping from his being. "It this dadgone sorry arm of mine. I jus' caint get used to not havin' it like it ought to be."

"Papa, the doctor said it might take a while to come back strong . . ."

"A while. Near a year? I jus' feel like a waste."

"I know, Papa, I see it in your eyes and the way you carry your head. But you ought not to think that way. You carry your weight. It work fine to trade off our jobs, long as they all get done." Truly, Solomon wanted only to help both of his parents but the weight of trading roles with his father and being the strongest, most capable person in the family would bury him if he let it. If he let that happen, his family would surely perish. *Got to stick to it long as it takes. Long as it takes . . .*

Moses explained, "I been workin' all afternoon on a stump in the new ground and got it dug 'round. But I caint pull the blasted thing out, even with Sudie and Sally, both of 'em."

Much too quickly Solomon said, "Well, if two mules can't pull the stump out, what am I supposed to do with it?" As soon as the words left his mouth, Solomon regretted them. Moses recoiled from his son's words.

"I'm sorry, Papa," Solomon offered, sitting on a stump near his father. "I didn't mean that like it sounded; I just don't know what to do if those old gals can't pull it out."

"I know, son. You workin' so hard these days, you meet yourself comin' and goin'. Way too much on a still growing boy." Moses drooped onto the chopping block and thought out loud. "Make a big difference to get them stumps out and plow through 'stead of 'round." Moses was defeated. "Jus' keep athinkin' that stump be out had I my arm full strength."

"Papa, listen to what you sayin'," Solomon said in a mix of sarcasm and hilarity. "Sally and Sudie can't pull that old stump out you ain't gon' do it one good arm or twenty."

"You right, boy. Jus' hard for a body to get old." He looked thoughtful. "Never thought 'bout it much -- gettin' old I mean -- but it start to jump, it jump on you hard."

"Look, Papa, we both worn slap out. Let's finish up chores today and ponder it. We'll go out tomorrow and see what we can figure." A good meal and rest would help them both, but the boy couldn't imagine they would find some magic answer. He just didn't have the heart to say more to his father.

Their quarters in Pete Harker's bunk house kept them dry and a few mosquitoes off them, but no extras. Even the lean-to had separate sleeping rooms and a fireplace to cook in. Lela was back to cooking on the outside fire pit, adding hundreds of extra steps for her every day. But then the bunk house was sturdier, less drafty, and much roomier than the house had been. It even had a real wood floor.

Solomon and Moses found little solution to their stump problem the next morning. The pine tree Moses had felled was huge and its tap root seemed to go as deep as the tree was tall. They had to cut it into three parts just so the mules could drag it to the house. Moses continued to clear another field so they could plant a bigger corn crop in the spring, but the work went slowly without full strength in the arm that took the bullet the year before.

Solomon continued chopping wood in a frenzy, knowing that there could never be too much wood and the cook fire was a wood-eating beast. The boy tried to have an outlook as cheerful as his mother's, but felt more harnessed to the hard dreary life of a farmer every day. It was midmorning and more to do than light left. As he led Sally toward the wood pile dragging yet another downed oak tree, Solomon muttered to his mule, about the only being he spoke to freely these days. "Garden's been good and Mama can make something good outta nothin'. Smoke house holdin' fair but we got to kill hogs first cold spell for winter else we go hungry for sure. We ain't been hungry much, girl, but meat's scarce and work overflowin'. I sure do hanker for a mess a catfish." His mouth was salivating by the time he and his mule reached the yard. Solomon untied the tree, unharnessed Sally, and left her to graze, knowing she wouldn't stray. "Yessir," he said to the mule, reaching for the fishing pole he'd not touched in weeks, "a good mess of catfish do my spirit some good. Won't do my belly no harm, either."

Lela realized that Solomon wasn't nearby but assumed he had gone to the field to help his father. Little Sarah squirmed on a pallet as Lela stirred the pot that hung over the old cook fire. She didn't need luxury, but Lela didn't look forward to cooking in the open through another winter, especially as days got shorter and shorter. Work had to last until final darkness so supper had to wait until after that. She stretched her back and wiped her brow before she lifted clothes, piece by piece, from the boiling hot wash water. "'Least this is the last of it," she sighed as she rinsed the soap out of the wash in a tub of clean water.

The wash would be hung tonight and dry before noon on the clothesline her men made for her. That had been a welcome improvement after too many laundry days spreading clothes on bushes all around the yard. Laundry hung and seeing to Sarah after every trip, she carried buckets full of wash water to pour sparingly over the newly sprouted fall vegetables – greens and onions so far. Water was far too precious to let a drop go to waste.

A few minutes of peace and rest were Lela's reward as she fed a very hungry Sarah who, thank the good Lord, was beginning to tolerate mashed or chewed food. That peace was interrupted by Solomon sneaking up behind her with a small string of fish in his hand and a huge smile on his face.

"Solomon Freeman!" she gasped with a start that made Sarah wail. "What you doin' sneakin' up on a body like that?"

"Sorry, Mama. I just couldn't help it." He held out bounty for her to admire. "I'll get these old devils dressed and in cold water till you figure what you want to do with 'em."

"I just didn't know you had gone fishing, son." She said as she calmed the baby. "Where's your papa? He needs your help, you know."

"I know, Mama. I bet I wasn't gone more 'n an hour and I just knew some fish would taste good for a change. I'll head back out soon's I get these boys cleaned."

"No need, boy," came a familiar sound from behind him. Moses had turned both mules into the lot and was drenched with sweat. "I got done what I could. Figured I come in and do what need to get done here since I lost my help."

Solomon knew that tone. He'd heard it often enough that it shouldn't still make his spine shiver. But it did. "Papa, I finished the part you told me and hoped fish would go good for supper after a long day." He planned to continue, but was interrupted.

"Trouble alway come from a good thought ain't it, boy?" His hands clinched and the steam was almost visible from Moses' ears. He also had more to say.

Lela stood and reached a gentle hand toward her husband. "Moses, there's no harm . . . "

"Lela," Moses spat. "This between me and the boy." He had never told Lela she couldn't speak before. She also knew Moses had never felt less a man before. "You know I can't git ever'thing need doing done by myself."

"I know you need more help right now, Papa," Solomon began.

"Oh, you right about that. The old man need lots of help." This was about far more than chores and Moses would say his piece or explode. "Ain't never been hurt so's I caint do the work. Never been to where I knowed a boy half growed could be more man than me." Moses crumpled to the bench and held his head in his hands. "An' ain't never not knowed how to handle my own son." Frustration just poured from the big man's spirit.

Solomon took a chance and sat next to his father. "Papa?" he began. "Papa, you ain't never been less than full man." Moses turned from his son. "Nothin' would happen here if you didn't decide it. This place don't run without you." Nothing Solomon said made any difference, but he couldn't stop and, though unintentional, he sounded almost angry. "Papa, you got shot protectin' Mama from those men."

Moses just shook his bowed head. Solomon stood. "Papa, you did what need be to save this place and Mama. Now you sayin' you wish you hadn't a done that?" Lela watched her son struggle to reach his father and loved them for what they both felt. "I don't 'spect so. You just stop and think. Can't no man do more than his best an' that's all I ever known you to do." The boy sat close to his father. "You're arm ain't yet healed up but you keep working with it I just know it will. We just keep on every day – just like we done since we got here four years ago – and we get through. Ain't no reason we can't still do it – together."

CHAPTER THREE

Moses and Solomon were at dead calm for a few days. Just when Lela thought that, this time, her men wouldn't bridge their silence, an ice breaker rumbled onto the place. "Well, I declare!" Lela looked up under the shade of her hand. "It's so late, I'd given up on you this year, Pete."

The tall, slender man broke from the small herd of cattle and rode right up to Lela at the clothesline. His long legs matched the stature of the magnificent horse he rode and there was a long whip coiled ominously next to his saddle. He stepped down with a casual grace, dropped the reins, and reached with uncommon familiarity for the bundle in the sling on her back. "Oh, Lela," he said as he gently coaxed the wriggling baby from her cocoon. "Look at this little angel." He cradled Sarah in his large arm and gazed into her face.

"Why, Pete Harker, I do believe you've held a baby before. You did that natural as breathing."

Nearly inaudibly, he said wistfully, "Yes, I've done this before." A commotion behind him interrupted his sadness and he turned to watch his men run the cows into a holding pen, an easy task as Pete had a larger crew than usual. With the two quick dogs now, even the men didn't have as much to do. Still gently rocking the baby in his arms, Pete turned back to Lela and registered the charred rubble. "My God, Lela. What happened here? Are Moses and Solomon alright?"

Lela assured him that they were safe and had squeaked by for the past months as she described the fire. She poured him a cup of coffee and took Sarah so he could drink it. When she told him they were in the bunk house, hoping he didn't mind he almost burst. "Mind? What I would mind is you thinking for a second that it wouldn't be the thing to do!" Walking toward the bunk house he assured her. "You did just the right thing. I'm glad it was here for you. The men and I can bunk under the trees a few nights and we'll get some changes put in right away." Before Lela could protest Pete continued thinking out loud. "Cut the space about in half – a little more to the house side than the bunk side. It should serve both purposes. Besides, we're only here a few nights at a time. It makes no sense standing empty." Pete called Slim over and, after hellos, they made a quick assessment of the building. The three were standing on the front porch when Moses returned from the field.

Hearty greetings and relief that the Freemans were safe rang through the yard and into the woods. Out of the corner of his eye Slim noticed that the two new men were hanging back – unhappily if their faces were read right. He whispered a word of warning to Angus. "Best watch those two. They just might need some of the same teachin' we needed when we first signed on with Pete."

Angus saw immediately what Slim meant. "Aye," he chuckled, "they'll either ken that lesson or we'll be short handed."

"You'd be right, friend," the big man observed. "Pete Harker ain't tolerated no nasty treatments that I've seen and I 'spect he won't start with those two."

"Nay," agreed Angus, his brogue thickening, as he watched the sullen men sit on a stump away from the rest of the party. "I felt dark hearts in them toward Manuel, but hoped to see them calm in a day or two. I have me doobts now." They rejoined the group keeping watchful eyes.

"I have good memories of this cookfire," Pete observed as he held Sarah comfortably in his lap.

"It ain't like the fireplace, but that don't stop Lela none, Pete, you know that," Moses said, sitting a little taller and grimacing as he stretched his shoulder.

Pete's sharp eye caught Moses' wincing. "Moses, that shoulder hasn't repaired, has it? Do you mind if I check something?" Pete stood, gently handed Sarah over to her mother, and began kneading the muscles and testing the arm's range of motion. "Does it hurt all the time, Moses?"

"Not 'xactly, Pete. More when I try to reach up er back. For'ard ain't too bad most times. But I sure ain't got no strength in it."

"I'm no doctor, but I've seen some injuries where you had to do certain exact movements over and over to get the injured part oiled up and strong again. Did the doctor see it?" "He did not," Lela huffed, her displeasure with her husband clear.

"Granny Ma and Lela worked on it. That 'bout good a doctorin' as a body could get."

An educated man, Harker was careful never to hold it over these friends so he spoke carefully. "I don't want to mislead you, but Cookie'll be along before long with the cook wagon and he might know something that will help."

"Mr. Cookie study doctoring, Pete?"

"No, Moses," Pete said solemnly, "not exactly, but the war taught a lot of us things we never thought we'd need to know." In a faraway voice he added, "And wish we hadn't learned."

"Mr. Cookie workin' out of a wagon now, Mr. Pete?" Solomon had settled the mules and sneaked up on the conversation.

Pete turned quickly to greet the boy. "Why, Solomon Freeman. You've grown a foot since last I saw you!" Their enthusiastic greeting was limited to manly handshakes and back-thumping, but their mutual affection was obvious. The reunion was cut short the minute Solomon spied the dogs sprawled and panting under a tree.

Pete laughed as he watched the boy with the dogs and Moses shook his head, saying, "I never see the like, Pete. That boy track and kill for food or settle and train most any critter he a mind to."

Pete answered, still laughing, "I knew he would like those old curs, but never thought to see them settled so quickly with a stranger. They don't trust anybody."

By sundown, the herd was confirmed to the corral and watered, a feast provided by Lela and Cookie devoured, and Cookie's inspection of Moses' arm and shoulder begun. Cookie's grin peeked through his wiry whiskers. "Moses, were I your doctor, I believe I would advise things like stretching low over a washboard and reaching high at the clothesline." Moses stared at the cook in complete disbelief. Cookie continued straight-faced. "Your regular chores don't make you move your arm like it needs to move and I can't think of anything that would flex you better."

"Washboard . . . clotheslines," Moses sputtered as the company chuckled. "I ain't got what I used to, but I kin do heap more than washday."

"I meant no insult, Moses," Cookie assured the man. "It's just your arm will heal faster and better if you stretch it very carefully in every direction. Stretchin', mind you, not heavy lifting. You can build up to weight after you know it'll move free."

"I don't see how washin' gonna get my arm no stronger. No sir, I surely don't," Moses explained.

In mock indignation Pete turned on Moses. "I don't know what makes you so special, Moses Freeman." Before

Moses could speak Pete continued. "Never thought I'd see the day you'd put your pride on a mountain. Seems I can remember the time it was just fine for me to do laundry in my recovery but you're too good for it."

Moses knew that Pete wasn't really angry, but he'd certainly made his point. "You right, Pete," Moses laughed wryly. "But I was hopin' for somethin' more 'n washin'."

Cookie continued his prescription. "When you're good and bendable, stack wood to build strength." Cookie pointed his finger in caution. "Not chopping, mind you. Let Solomon or one of our men do that. You just pick up firewood as it's cut . . . just so." Cookie picked up a piece of nearby firewood, slowly raised his arm, and held it straight in front of him. He lowered it just as deliberately as he had raised it, then pulled his arm in and lifted the wood by flexing his elbow upward. "That's to build up the strength, don't you see?"

Moses made no effort to hide his skepticism in Cookie's exercise regimen, but knowing Lela wouldn't allow otherwise, he agreed to try it for a few days.

Moses did his regular chores but pitched in on wash day, too. Had anyone pressed him, he would have admitted that he had enjoyed spending that time with Lela and Sarah. The best thing was that after about a week he knew he had eased her load significantly and that was a satisfying feeling. The proud man also had to admit that Cookie might have known his doctoring after all. It wasn't normal, but his shoulder moved more freely and with less pain than it had since he'd been shot in the raid the previous year.

On the last night with the Freemans, Cookie shooed Lela from her own cook fire and dished up an excellent fire roasted ham dinner. Most of the company strolled off to after-dinner smokes, bedrolls, or walks after the big dinner. The Freemans and senior members of the crew stared into the waning fire just trying to breathe after eating so much.

Pete was uncharacteristically quiet. He and Moses were well beyond beating around the bush and Moses broke the silence. "Pete, you mighty quiet. Somethin' on your mind special?"

Lela joined the group as Pete's eyes went from one to the other of the Freemans. "Yes, Moses, there is, and best to be out with it now."

The Freemans leaned in a little because Pete sounded so serious. "Obviously, since we came in with cows, it's time for another drive to Way Key. Past time really, almost too late in the year to head out." All eyes were on Pete as he continued. "I'm working on a new venture – heck, it's no secret. I'm trying to open a bank in Madison."

"A bank?" Moses' admiration was evident. "You got that much money, Pete?"

"Moses! You don't ask a man how much money he has. Not even Pete," Lela whispered.

Laughing and relaxing a little, Pete explained. "Lela, it's fine. There's nobody in this life I trust more. If I can't be open with you, I'll never be open with anybody." He sat to give the details. "The answer to your question is no. I don't have all that much money, but I do have enough to get backers to help me start the bank. And we need a bank in this part of the state."

Solomon was wide-eyed. Moses wiped his brow. "Pete, we never had use for a bank. Don't have no money, don't need no bank," Moses said, laughing at his little joke. "But we be pullin' for you."

"Thank you, Moses. I hope the Freemans will be some of my very first depositors," Pete said seriously. "At any rate, I must spend several weeks in Savannah right now or I'll miss my chance. That means the drive goes without me." Pete inhaled slowly and deeply, then looked directly at Solomon. "He's experienced two drives to Way Key and, naturally, I want Solomon to go on this one. As a matter of fact, I want him to lead it."

Solomon's eyes couldn't have gotten bigger, Moses wrung his hat so tightly it wouldn't open back up by itself, and Lela's gasp revealed her fear for her son. It was Solomon who spoke. "Pete, that's a fine, nice thing you sayin'. But, Mr. Cookie or Slim or Manuel or Angus could sure do better than me."

Before Pete could answer, Cookie interrupted. "No, son, we don't think so. You should know that Pete talked with us about this whole idea and we agree with him. All four of us."

Slim nodded and Angus said, "Aye, lad, aye," to confirm Cookie said was true. Manuel's big grin said he was in complete agreement.

"It's a big job," Cookie continued, "but in just two drives Solomon learned more about cows, horses, and makin' deals than we know all together. Most of the men have worked with Solomon and the new ones can see right quick who's boss."

"Cookie's right," Pete continued. "Lela, if you squeeze your hands together any harder, they'll break. Now, just calm down and believe that we've thought this through." Moses' reaction told Lela that he'd hadn't known this was coming either. She tried to stay calm, but it wasn't easy for a mother not to worry.

Solomon followed the conversation through a haze of shock. Pete spoke directly to Moses and Lela. "After his safety, your first concern is probably Solomon's ability to lead a drive. Believe me, we've spent hours answering that very question. I've never seen anyone of any age learn new skills as quickly as Solomon does. And once learned he doesn't forget lessons. I think you know these men will do everything they can to help and protect Solomon."

For the first time in his life, Pete Harker wished that he had become the lawyer his father had wanted. If he had, he might feel more confident in his arguments for Solomon's case. "Now, Lela, I've hinted Solomon taking extra responsibility to Moses, but not specifically this. Though he's not convinced, he said he would listen. I hope you will, too, before you pass judgment." Lela's head inclined and brow arched imperceptibly, daring Pete to offer an argument strong enough to convince her to let her baby face such a huge challenge. "I've seen lots of men in high pressure situations try to lead others and had to learn pretty fast how to do it myself. But I've never seen anyone -- any age -- with better natural wisdom for decision making and working with others. I believe that Solomon can do this successfully and without harm to himself or the crew or I'd never be mentioning it."

The last assurance Pete gave the Freemans was that he had purposely brought extra men along so that a couple of them could stay at the farm to make up for Solomon's absence. "There's always lots to be done on a place, but there's even more reason to leave a couple of extra men here is getting that bunk house in order. A couple of loads of saw timber and a few days' work and you'll have rooms, windows, and all the comforts of a real house. It'll be up to Lela to make it a home and there's nobody who can do that better."

Pete had said all he could think of to say. It was up to Moses and Lela now. Moses stretched his back and put his arm around Lela protectively. "Pete," Moses said, "we thank you for your trust in our boy. It's a real fine compliment. Me and Lela, we talk on it and I 'spect we pray on it some and when we find our answer we let you know."

Turning toward the silent young man across the fire from him, Moses added, "Son, you sat quiet here. Not spoke up 'tall. Shows control I didn't know you had and that good. Me and your Mama know your wish be to go and we do our best to think on it fair for you."

CHAPTER FOUR

Solomon was up before dawn, having slept little. When he got to the cook fire, he saw that he wasn't the only restless one. He took the steaming coffee Moses offered. "You didn't sleep much, Papa."

"No," Moses replied, shaking his head, "guess I didn't." The man motioned for his son to sit. Pouring another cup of coffee for himself, sat on a log and stared into the dark, strong brew. Finally he spoke. "Me and your mama knows you want to go. That right?"

"Yessir, I think I do." Afraid to say too much at once, Solomon waited.

"We talk a lot and pray a lot last night. 'Specially with Pete leavin' some help while the drive on, guess ain't no reason for you not to."

Solomon wasn't sure whether he should celebrate or hold on for the rest for surely there was more. He held still. "Thank you, Papa. You know I don't want to do somethin' you don't give leave to do. But, I do want to try. I think I can do this, Papa. I really think I can."

Moses shook his head slowly and flexed his stiff arm. "Don't know just how, but I believe you can do it, too, son. You got to be fair and work hard as you do here. Maybe most men might take to you in the lead, but it be a mite hard for some to be takin' orders from a colored boy." Solomon nodded

solemnly. His father, who almost never spoke to him man-to-man like this, had more to say. "You got to make them men and them cows the most main thing. You jus' think on things and act with them men 'stead of bossin' 'em."

"Yessir, Papa," was the breathless reply. "I'll remember surely."

The next day, the company assembled around the cook fire. Plans were set and people knew their parts, but it seemed that somebody needed to say something or they'd stand there 'til noon waiting to go their ways.

Moses stepped up, hand extended to Pete. "This the big day I reckon, Pete. Our boy takin' somethin' on might be bigger 'n him. Time tell on that. I give him the best I could. Told him he need to respect his men and work 'long side 'em 'stead of over 'em."

Pete spoke what reflected in the experienced drovers' faces. "Moses, that's all any man can hope to do. It's exactly what I have always tried to do." A final handshake sealed the confidence they had in each other and in Solomon.

Pete mounted, and rode north on Diamond. "He knew all along he wasn't going on this drive, Papa," said Solomon. "That's why he rode Diamond instead of Hambone."

"Reckon so, son." Moses was even quieter than usual like he always was when something was burning on his mind. "Reckon it be your time to head on, too, son," the man said without moving.

But Solomon didn't go. The two men turned slowly and looked at each other straight and hard. No more words were needed. They nodded their heads and Solomon turned to mount the only good kind of horse for such a journey – his marshtackie, Swamp Foot.

The crew tightened the herd as Solomon rode toward his mother who held baby Sarah. This time Solomon held out his arm to take his mother's delicate hand. Words had either already been said or were so deeply felt that they didn't need to be said because, again, parent and child didn't speak. With a final squeeze of Lela's hand and a hand to Sarah's cheek, Solomon wheeled Swamp Foot and headed south with the herd.

The two men Pete left to help the Freemans in Solomon's absence moved a little closer, but not close enough to be considered sociable. Moses and Lela stood so close they appeared as one being. Lela was the first to speak after the dust settled. "He's making a fine man, Moses." She turned to look up at her giant of a husband. "The picture isn't what we might have ordered up, but he's growing into his own kind of man."

"No," Moses rasped. "Reckon it time to know he ain't bein' contrary. He just bein' hisself." Dumping the subject and the mood with a hard shake of his head, Moses directed, "Lela, honey, you been scurryin' 'round all mornin' and you tuckered out." He held up his hand. "No ma'am, no arguin'. You see to Sarah and take some rest in the shade a while."

Lela, hating to admit that Moses was right, wearily made her way to a low bench under an oak canopy. The fed Sarah, leaned against the tree trunk,
and joined Sarah in a much needed nap. As much as Sarah was thriving, Lela hadn't regained her strength after the little girl's birth. Lela attributed that to the unusual number of years between Solomon's birth and Sarah's.

As Moses moved toward Harry and Shorty they weren't sure what to do next. Neither was Moses. "Well, Moses," Shorty began hestitantly, "lots of day left and prob'ly lots to do. What would you have me and Harry do first?"

Moses realized he would have to take the very advice he had given Solomon. He would have to work with these men and never try to boss them. Especially since he could tell they weren't keen on being his help. "I say first, gent'men, we all go get a good store of cool spring water. It too hot to be workin' dry."

The men looked puzzled but walked with Moses to the spring branch where each man drank his fill and doused his face and neck with icy, clear spring water. By the time they were refreshed and ready to work, the directions had been decided. Moses would hitch up Sudie and break up what was left of the old corn field after harvest. Turning to the two aloof men Moses said, "You men know better'n me what Pete would have you do 'n that prob'ly plenty of work. Should I hit mor'n a one man job I be shore to ask you."

Harry and Shorty shrugged, nodded and moved toward the pile of saw timber they'd brought in from New Troy the day before. First, they would tackle renovations on the bunk house with every intention of the job taking a very long time. As soon as Moses was out of earshot, Harry started. "Least we ain't gotta work just right 'long side that darkie. Ain't much here I seen yet that I like 'n don't know as I'm gon' find anything." The shifty man rubbed his stubbly beard. "Though got to admit that little coffee-and-cream woman is a tolerable sight."

Shorty had been afraid of this. He turned on his companion and glared into the hard man's eyes. "Look, Harry. This is how it is. Pete pays good wages. Better 'n most. This ain't my first choice neither, but I made the agreement with Pete and my family needs the money." He spoke slowly and clearly for emphasis. "You can't handle it, go on and get gone. I don't plan on breakin' up any ruckus and don't plan on them Freemans giving Pete a bad account of me."

"Humph!" Harry snorted. "I ain'ta leavin' – least not just yet. I'm willin' to give it a chance. But them darkies get too chummy, I'll leave it and Pete can pay me when he sees me in Madison."

For most of the day Harry and Shorty worked in cool cooperation. They spoke when necessary to get the job done, worked separately when they could, and stopped a few times for a cool drink before returning to the bunk house job.

Finally, Harry breached the uneasy air when he observed, "At leas' the woman ain't set to tellin' us how to do this."

"Well, no, I don't 'magine she needs to after all the directions Pete gave us," Shorty retorted.

"Beatin'est thing I ever saw." Shorty removed his wide brimmed hat and wiped his forehead with his shirt tail. "Never thought I'd see the likes of Pete Harker with his schooling and high ways and all mixin' so freely with such as these Freemans."

"I sure don't have answers for you. Why don't you just question Pete on that when next you see him," Harry punctuated his message as he spat brown tobacco juice out of the newly cut window and turned back to its window sill.

A couple of cold biscuits had done for lunch, but by supper time Harry and Shorty were both so hungry they would have eaten anybody's cooking. Besides, when it came to cooking Lela Freeman was not just anybody. The one thing the two reluctant carpenters had to admit was that they weren't likely to suffer from lack of food. The stores Pete left there would assure that. And not just food – it was good food under Lela's hands.

What they weren't so sure about sitting around the same cook fire, eating from the very same tin plates the Freemans ate from. "They been washed. Just eat," snapped Shorty quietly when Harry muttered his reluctance.

Eat they did. At least they both had enough wits to thank Lela for the meal. As soon as they could, though, they got their bed rolls from the bunk house so they could sleep at a distance from it. Pete paid them well to follow his orders but that didn't mean they were going to actually live with these people.

CHAPTER FIVE

Solomon must have almost turned back a dozen times in the first few days. He doubted that he could live up to the faith Pete had in him. He didn't want to worry or disappoint his parents. The men did as he said, but he could tell they were nervous, too. To most eyes, putting the safety of the herd and the drovers in the hands of a fifteen-year-old boy wasn't a good gamble -- a colored boy, at that.

Different from the previous two drives, Cookie and the wagon stayed on the rude roadways that cut through the territory. Half the men stayed with the increasing herd and moved along near the wagon while the other half split off to either side bringing in an odd assortment of woods cows. Solid, spotted, and brindle cows of all ages lumbered restlessly into the fold. Some moved in smoothly while others were skittish for a few days before settling. Once in a while a critter remained so ornery that it was encouraged to return to the wild. As long as they didn't run the herd too tightly the cows were manageable.

Over a typical supper of beans and biscuits near the end of the first week, Slim put a voice to Solomon's thinking. "Solomon, ain't no question none of us was too keen on this new way of huntin'."

A twinkle in his eye betraying his increasing comfort, Solomon asked, "Now, Slim, would that be the plan for me to be boss or the plan to keep more to the roads?"

For an instant, a couple of new men held their breath for fear of Slim's slow, but well known temper. Slim cocked his head and squinted at Solomon. Then he burst into laughter with as much gusto as he delivered a temper fit. "Young Solomon, that would be a good question. A good question for sure." He made a show of scratching his head and continued. "Mebbe I mean botha them plans!"

The company relaxed and Slim continued. "I been with Pete Harker long enough to know he mostly thinks on things enough to get 'em right. And I was one of them agreed with him mostly. Got to say, though, I was just a fraction afraid he wasn't thinkin' straight when he turned things over to you." Slim shook his head and held up a hand. "No, it weren't that I wanted to be boss. Nosirreebob. I do just fine bein' number two."

Cookie chuckled and ribbed the big man. "So, Slim, tell us just what your problem is with our new boss. You got trouble findin' the right words?"

Rolling his eyes at Cookie's "help" Slim tried to find the elusive right words. "Well now, after a few days in the saddle I saw you might take to the leadin' pretty fair. Oh, you got things to learn, but me and Cookie here, and the other boys'll fill you in when you need to be told. It's this stayin' with the road thing I was really speakin' of." All ears were perked up to see how Slim would say what they knew would be correction. "Yessir, everybody knows cows don' travel on no roads. What possesses a body to think we find 'em woods cows any place besides in the deep woods?" Heads bobbed in agreement demonstrating that not all of the crew had accepted Solomon and some were just waiting to watch him fail.

"Well," Slim explained sheepishly, "seem you think on things 'bout like Pete does. Cookie ain't far case somebody needs some doctorin' but moves faster on the roads – even bad ones – than winding through the woods. Him going a little ahead and pickin' the night's camp gets him there afore us and the cows."

Close observation would have revealed a couple of disappointment-stricken faces when they realized Slim didn't plan to berate Solomon at all. Cookie struck up the next part of the conversation. "Slim, I been thinking that very same thing. Me gettin' to the camp first lets me set up and start supper before the cows come along and muddy the river. That way the men can work a little longer in the day and pull in more cows. And you got to admit the food's a sight better than when we pack supplies."

"'Tis a comfort to approach camp of an evening to the fire's bouquet," said Angus, his brogue still Highland thick. "Knowin' that the coffee is hot and," he shot a grin across the fire at Cookie, "the beans – since that be the name our venerable cook gives that substance which is oft' times mush and elsewise pebbles – ready to fill our bellies."

Cookie gave a loud, "Hurrumph!" in protest though he knew Angus was pulling his leg. "Well, Mister MacDougal," Cookie said in gentle mockery, "I cannot tell you how glad I am that my efforts do not go unnoticed."

Slim took the lead again sternly. "What I mean to say, Solomon, is that you done a good thing. We collectin' more cows quicker than before and givin' enough time for the cookin' seein' as how I most rather eat mush than rocks."

"Sí, Señor Slim," said Manuel in improving English. "Our young Solomon is *no niño no mas*. He learn so fast because he have good *professores*." The original crew congratulated each other for being outstanding teachers while the new men looked at each other in puzzlement. They didn't understand these relationships at all.

"I thank you, Mr. Slim. And the rest of you, too." Solomon knew it was time for his first real speech to the men. He also knew he had no idea what to say. "You not the only ones been worried 'bout my bossin'. I don't even like the sound of that word – boss. Ain't what I'm tryin' to do anyhow." Solomon's hat was now being wadded up in his anxious hands.

The Boss took a deep breath an continued. "All I want is to get this drive done and finished and get us back to the farm safe and with good money for Mr. Pete. I know I still got to learn and . . . well . . . ain't no pride in me keeps me from listenin' to better men than me. I'll thank you for stayin' close to help me figure on things. And I hope I don't let a one of you down." Solomon's eyes scanned the circle of men – the whole crew except the three riding the night watch – and saw little disagreement or resentment, at least on the surface. "We all put in a hard day and eat our fill of Mr. Cookie's good cookin'. I'm thinkin' next watch come soon enough and mornin' soon after that so we best to find our blankets."

Solomon was so relieved to have gotten through his little speech that he didn't notice the approval signaling among Slim, Cookie, Angus, and Manuel or the simmering resentment in Murphy and George, two new men. Charlie One-Hand, as he was now called, had been silent during the talking and continued to watch the new hands with concern. He made it his quiet mission to keep an extra eye on them.

The way the cow hunters wound around and about, it wasn't easy to travel directly to Captain Dudley's place. Between prospecting for the scattered bovines and weaving through natural obstacles, nothing was found on a straight line.

The herd made its now routine stop at Camp Sink and settled in for a couple days' rest before the drive moved hard south. It took most of the drovers to mind the herd and little camp, so only Solomon, Slim, and Big Jim rode on to the Dudley's.

Mary Dudley was reserved but Solomon knew she was considerably more welcoming than the Captain would be. She directed the small band to the well to cool off as a boy about Solomon's age took their horses to water.

Solomon knew that if Pete had been along, the picture would've been different. Recognizing Pete's obvious attachment to Solomon, Mrs. Dudley would have allowed him to join Pete on the front porch for cold lemonade or cider. As it was, the men were invited to the well with the young trail boss.

The well was behind the house and, as they splashed cold clear well water on their faces, Solomon voiced his observations to his companions. "I don't wonder you both might be enjoyin' a cool drink on the porch if Pete was here."

Slim, reading Solomon's thoughts assured him, "Now that just ain't so, boy. Pete woulda found a fine seat in one of them rockin' chairs, but don't none of us equal him." Through water droplets falling from his soaked hair, Slim knew his trail boss recognized false praise so he was always open and honest. "Nope. You just can't get all worried up about if Pete was here."

Big Jim, who had already learned to respect Solomon far more than he would ever have predicted, offered his encouragement. "Slim's right, Solomon." Taking his first opportunity to be part of the old core crew, Big Jim hiked up his britches and stretched as tall as his wiry five feet and four inch height would let him and continued. "I ain't knowed him long but what I see of Pete Harker he ain't making no careless judgments it comes to business." Leaning on the edge of the well wall, his freckles popping out red in the heat, he became philosophical. "Mind you I ain't suggestin' Pete's greedy. He ain't gon' let his belief get turned for money. But, he ain't careless 'bout business neither."

"You're right on that, Jim," said Slim seriously.

"No, I'd say Pete made you boss because he knowed you the best man for the job. He put it in your hands and knowed you do just fine by him."

Solomon deeply appreciated the support of these two men. One he had known several years and the other just weeks, but they had something in common that they probably didn't know Solomon was aware of. At first neither man was happy about working any place near people they thought probably should still be slaves. On top of that, this darkie was just a stripling. Their loyalty demonstrated that those feelings were long gone. "I hear what you're saying, both of you. And I thank you for trying to make this right. But, you know well as me that this whole drive would run different if Pete was here like he ought to be."

Pouring a final dipper of water over his curly ebony hair, Slim agreed. "Good and true point, son. But that be the case no matter which one of us he put in charge." He wiped his face and shook his head slightly. "I don't know all the rush about being in Savannah, but he wasn't making this drive no matter what."

"That's the truth, Solomon," chimed Big Jim. "He said as much on the way to your place."

"I admit," Slim said softly, "he spoke of me taking it on if it didn't work for you to do it." Solomon was relieved that there was Plan B. "Nope. I told Pete straight that wasn't for me. I know cows; known 'em all my life. But I ain't got no head for making deals and don't get along near as good with men as I do with cows." Shaking his head and wiping his thick hair straight back with his hands Slim went on. "Boss has to be full boss, Solomon. Can't do just part of the job and you doing just fine for us."

"Well, we've gotten this far, but there's been no big dealing either." Solomon shook his lowered head doubtfully. "I got to say I'm pure scared about fixin' a deal with Captain Dudley. He was through and through Reb and I ain't sure that's changed a whole lot. Even the ships' captains might be easier than him."

The two drovers nodded in agreement with Solomon and pledged they would do all they could to help him succeed. The young trail boss took a final sip then doused his head with water. He continued rubbing his face as though he might wash away his insecurities if he just rubbed hard and long enough. Removing his hands, Solomon saw a pair of bare feet. They were long and slender -- almost delicate -- but calloused, proof of a lifetime of hard work. He raised his drenched head, wiping the remaining water from his eyes and realized that, offering him a mason jar of cool sweet sour orange juice was a girl who matched her feet. Tall, slender, nearing dainty. As with her feet, though, it was clear that there was grit hidden in that lean body.

Slim and Big Jim were already holding similar jars and watched to read Solomon's response. His feet shifted nervously and he took the refreshment from her outstretched hand. "Thank you," Solomon croaked. "Thank you kindly."

The girl, whose stare hadn't left the jar she held, bolted her eyes on Solomon's when his hand brushed hers took a half step back and murmured, "I'm Sally Mae." Before Solomon could breathe, she was gone -- disappearing behind the smokehouse.

Slim and Big Jim grinned at each other, but before they could rib their boy boss with his mouth still gaping, an arrival interrupted. Captain P. B. H. Dudley was home. With Mrs. Dudley's direction, the big man passed straight through the dog trot and out the back door toward the well. Looking down on the men from the porch, he stopped short. "I 'spected you a week ago. You must be finding a passel of cows." He squinted with distrust as he moved toward them. "Where'd you leave Pete?"

There was nothing Slim wanted to do more than step right up and speak for Solomon, but if the boy didn't stand for himself now things would go all wrong. Clearing his throat Solomon spoke. "Mr. Pete's not with us this trip, Cap'n Dudley, sir." Despite all the refreshment he'd had Solomon felt like his throat had dried and stuck to itself. "And we intended to be here 'least a few days ago, but you know cows don't line up straight for you to just pluck them up. Had to do some huntin'."

He'd let the boy step up and speak first, but Slim just had to try to help out. He extended his hand and said boldly, "Good seein' you, Cap'n. This here's a new man Big Jim Hanson."

Dudley took one look at Big Jim, threw back his head, and let out a belly laugh. "**Big** Jim? Ain't that a sight?"

Jim had heard it all before and just stepped right up to meet the man who towered over him. "Yessir, Cap'n, suppose my mama thought maybe I might grow into the name if'n I was give it." He shrugged his shoulders and sparked a big smile. "Reckon she was wrong!" Dudley had to catch his breath before he could shake hands and kept glancing at the little man and chuckling.

Suddenly, Dudley put his hat back on his head with purpose and turned to Solomon, all smiles gone. "I can't see Pete putting Big Jim in charge, him a new man and all. Slim ain't much stepped up to do it." His eyes bored into Solomon's soul. "You ain't tellin' me you in charge."

"Yessir, Cap'n. Mr. Pete asked me to build the herd this year and things goin' right good so far. Besides the woods cows, we made agreement with two farmers on the way for their market beef." The boy hoped that would suggest to Dudley that he didn't need to be the first hiccup of the drive. "Plan is to rest up to Camp Sink at least two days while we bringin' up your stock then move on south."

"The plan is, eh?" Dudley didn't quite know what to think of this unexpected development, except that he didn't much like it. "I'll miss parleying with Cap Harker, yessir I will. He's a good man can drive a good bargain. Well, you men know where to bunk and supper'll be at the back porch in a while. Maybe we'll talk on the morn." His emphasis on the word men was unmistakable. The way he saw things, he was talking to two drovers and a colored boy.

There wasn't much conversation as the drovers checked on their horses and put their gear in the little storeroom that served as guest quarters for such as them. It was a long night of tossing, turning, and speech practicing for Solomon.

"Slim," he said at first light, "what if the Cap'n don't bring up dealing? What if he just sort of passes the whole thing by? We can't wait here more than a day or so and the others deserve a chance to come through the store here. We'd just have to shove on with or without his stock."

"You right about that," responded Slim in a croak that told Solomon his second in command hadn't slept much either. "You gonna have to do the talking' and dealin' but I ain't a mind to let you do it by yourself." On his feet and rolling his bedroll, "I don't aim to butt in, mind you, you got to do the speaking, but I ain't chancing him takin' advantage neither."

They needn't have worried about wasting time. By the time they'd had a cup of coffee and a couple of biscuits, Dudley approached looking serious. "Let's be about it, here. No secret I ain't keen on this arrangement." Leaning against a barn wall, Dudley took out a sharp knife and began to whittle casually. "But, seeing how Pete Harker put stock in you, I don't have a lot of choice.

Saved my market stock for him to pick up and can't afford to lose time finding other deals." Dudley knew Solomon must be jumpy nervous inside but, to his credit, the boy appeared fairly calm. "Nope, got to deal now, I suppose."

Feeling the need to say something before Dudley felt he could just do all of the talking and run right through him, Solomon stood straight and said, "Well, sir, I'm sure you got prime animals ready chosen. Mr. Pete says of the whole trip, it' the Dudley stock that bring the herd up to sellin' prices."

"He does, does he?" Dudley said, surprised with the boy's approach. "What you authorized to offer, Mr. Trail Boss?"

"Can't never know what we get from the docks," Solomon answered, hoping his voice wasn't as shaky as his guts. "You know Pete Harker shoots straight. Don't imagine he's ever shortchanged a man in his life. Least I wouldn't think so." This was it. If Solomon didn't do this next part right, they could be short a full shipload of cows. "I reckon the plan would be to what we've always done – take a count and move on to Way Key. We keep every tally separate – each one like you who send their stock and the woods cows on Pete's tally -- and divide any trail loss equal."

Dudley just kept whittling as though he expected Solomon to say more. The glint of sun on steel nearly paralyzed the boy boss. The silence was awkward making Slim want to step in but he didn't. Solomon finished explaining the plan that he knew Dudley already knew. "On the way back through we stop at every place we got cows and pay off according to record."

His knife slipped a mite and Dudley raised his head expectantly. "Straight pay-off then."

"No sir, Captain, can't take that back to Mr. Pete." Solomon was careful to be formal and respectful using Sir or Captain and Mr. Pete instead of the familiar Pete he normally used. Dudley's short humph told the boy to continue. "No sir, we got to cover drovers' pay and supplies, too."

Dudley and Harker had conducted their business in private and Dudley surmised that Solomon might not be too well informed about those dealings. "I suppose that's a point all right," Dudley admitted, adding a sharp point on the end of his whittling stick. He continued talking as he tested the spiky end of the stick with only a hint of menace. "I'd think twenty percent would cover all the expenses and that'd make Pete's woods herd all profit."

Solomon shook his head thoughtfully. "No, sir. Expenses run more than that for sure and this year we got hands enough you don't have to lose the time of two of your men." Solomon knew he must be out with it now or lose the battle here. "I think Mr. Pete had more in mind something like forty percent."

The whittle stick pierced the ground between their feet a little closer to Solomon's than Dudley's. "The hell you say, boy. The hell you say." Dudley shook his head in mock disbelief and countered, "Ain't no expenses up to that. I'll go twenty-five. Chew on that." He then turned the knife to cleaning under his fingernails.

Big Jim, having finished saddling their horses, stood on the edge of the group behind Slim, whose neck tendons were stretched about as tight as it was possible to stretch them. Jim noticed the big man's clinched fists, too, and hoped the negotiations weren't going as badly as it appeared.

Solomon slumped against the barn's hitching rail and clinched his lips in defeat. "Cap'n, you got quality animals. I know that without even seein' 'em or knowin' how many you aiming to send with us. But I also know a crew can't run on that. We got to have thirty percent or just go on and try to see you again next year." The boy stood up, looked directly into Dudley's squinted eyes, and just stared.

After a minute of the two trying to read each other' thoughts, Dudley finally stepped forward, popping the knife closed and ramming it into his pocket. "Thirty percent? Don't see how you got the brass to tell me it takes thirty percent to run a drive. I just can't see it." The man paused. The boy didn't turn away. "Oh hell, boy, I can't hold these cows over another year. Ain't got the winter feed for the whole herd. Get mounted and we'll see how many the men have cut from the herd."

Big Jim stopped holding his breath. Slim let his rigid muscles relax. Solomon thought he was going to collapse from nerves and relief. Either that or puke. There was no luxury of time, though, if they were to keep up with Dudley and maintain their position. He turned to his men. "Slim. Big Jim. After the count, you ride on back to the herd and send three more of the crew to come for half the day. Three more can come after them."

CHAPTER SIX

The count done, the three cow hunters walked to the corral so Slim and Big Jim could return to Camp Sink, leaving Solomon on his own until the next group could get there. As the drovers walked past the back of the barn, Solomon noticed a slender figure pressed up against the building. This time he noticed that her hair was shorn, following the shape of her head. He'd not seen that style on a woman but he didn't find it unappealing. As his head turned toward her, he saw almond shaped eyes just before the figure turned and dashed out of sight.

As Solomon watched the men ride away he was washed in the most powerful sense of loneliness he had ever felt. Every nerve in his body seemed afire and his head hurt. Not on the outside like it did several years before when the tree fell on him during the hurricane, but inside, like muffled drums. He meandered away from the Dudley place and into the woods as naturally as breathing. It would have been impossible for him to tell how far he had walked or how long it took him to get where he was.

Someone coming upon him would have thought he had sat under the tree and fallen asleep sitting up, but his eyes weren't closed and his muttering was barely audible. "Too much. Ain't never should have let Pete talk me into this." Then the monologue went the opposite direction. "No, it's my fault. My own fault altogether. I wanted to get away. Had to get away from the load at home. See how that worked out; got a load way bigger than home now." His muttered thoughts changed directions again. "How could Pete think I could do this? And the others did, too. I can't . . ."

Through blurry eyes, Solomon saw a beautiful head wrapped in a yellow scarf sitting silently by him – just watching him. Solomon stood so quickly he jolted the young woman. Pacing four steps one way, four the other, he didn't know where he was going. He rubbed his head and face to wipe away the dread he felt.

She stood and caught his hands. She wasn't holding them hard but he was powerless to pull away and rub off whatever was making his skin crawl. He looked into her upturned eyes and felt calm course through his body. Blinking hard, he asked, "What did you do? What did you do to me?"

Her head pulled back at the accusation but she stood firm. "Nothin'. I didn't do nothin' to you more'n try to hear and help a body I thought could be my friend."

Solomon's mouth opened and closed like a puppet with no words. "Don't be feared, Mr. Freeman. I ain't no harm to you," she whispered as her hand rested on his shoulder with a feather's touch. Again calm flowed through his body and the pair sat as if in a dream.

"Sallie Mae? Isn't that it? Sallie Mae?"

"Yes, I Sallie Mae." Solomon wiped the last of the stupor from his eyes, leaning heavily against the tree. Sallie sat in front of him, ramrod straight, their knees nearly touching and looked straight through him. "And you be troubled. Your demons stirrin'"

"Huh? What?" Solomon sputtered. "What does that mean – my demons? That's just crazy talk."

"No, not crazy – true. I see it in your eyes and I hear you talkin' to yourself."

"You . . . you . . . you followed me?"

For the first time, Sallie Mae was flustered. "Oh, no, Mr. Freeman. When I done with my chores I walks all over these woods, I do. Know every corner near 'bout. Ever'body know when they caint find me I's someplace in these woods."

"Who was I talking to? I don't know why I'm so discombobulated." Solomon was less in control of himself than he could ever remember.

"You been sleepin' poorly?" Solomon nodded. "It show in your eyes. They red. And you ain't standin' straight and proud like when I first seen you bringing cows through before." Sally Mae looked down at her clinched hands. "And

. . . I didn't mean to over listen you but I feared you was sick or somethin' you acted so strange. Kind of a dreamlike way."

"You said I talked. What did I say?"

Sallie Mae and Solomon slowly wound their way back toward Dudley, stopping when their conversation was most intense. Sallie Mae tried to explain to Solomon what she had heard and what he sounded like as he wandered and mumbled. Some of it made sense to Solomon and he explained his fighting feelings of adventure and fear.

As they approached the edge of the woods they instinctively stopped. Something changed and they both fidgeted and looked at their feet. "Sallie Mae," Solomon said quietly, "I'm not real sure what's happenin' in my mind but I'm thanking you for being there. I guess I needed a friend and I feel settled more than since I left home."

"You most welcome, Mr. Freeman." She raised her hands all but touching his cheeks and unblinkingly peered into his eyes. Warmth and calm radiated through his entire body. After a few seconds she dropped her hands. With a small smile she added, "I best git back 'n you come different way. I ain't askin' for no loose talk 'bout me."

"Couldn't be loose talk about you, Sallie Mae," he assured her gently, "but it's a good idea. I'll circle around and come in from a different direction." He spoke in a whisper as though revealing a great mystery. "We'll be headin' on south day after, but do you think we could talk again tomorrow?" The shy young man held his breath.

Eyes sparking, the girl answered, "My chores take up the morning time for sure. Times I get away usually after lunch time."

She took a step to leave the woods and he touched her shoulder gently. "And Sallie Mae – it's Solomon. My Papa is Mr. Freeman."

She hadn't even turned to look at him but he saw her acceptance in her posture as she walked out of sight.

CHAPTER SEVEN

Lela found herself with only baby Sarah for company. Shorty and Harry were in New Troy picking up a final wagon load of lumber for the bunk house renovations and Moses was in the woods beyond the corn field. She took full advantage of the quiet and lack of interruption to get the house in order. There were still scraps of lumber and saw dust all over the place. But there were improvements to be sure.

The place already had a full wood floor that was almost level. Pure extravagance for certain was the overhang that now extended the length of the building covering a generous porch and making it look like the front of a proper house. Shorty, a good hand with carpentry, built several straight back chairs. "Rockers is a might 'bove me," he had explained apologetically to Lela. She hadn't cared a whit, and the porch soon became her favorite place. As a matter of fact, as soon as she finished inside, she would sit there and do hand work.

As she put Sarah down for a nap, Lela chuckled quietly remembering how her own personal chair had come about. So happy just to have sturdy chairs, she never would have complained, but as Shorty walked from the cook fire toward the corral to do a final check on the horses he noticed something odd. Moses' chair was leaned on its back legs and his big feet were propped up on a porch post. Solomon wasn't there, but he'd do fine in the chairs. It was Lela who caught his eye. Her feet didn't touch the floor. They didn't even almost touch the floor. The man whom Lela was sure didn't really want to be there approached the porch sheepishly and said, "Ma'm, I ain't meanin' no familiarity, but that chair got to be fixed." Moses sat square and eyed the man suspiciously. Lela looked confused.

"Whatever do you mean, Mr. Shorty. These are just about the sturdiest chairs I've ever seen. We're most grateful for them and have you to thank."

"No. Pardon ma'am," he explained, "I got to measure how much leg to cut offa that one you're sittin' in. Ain't no good your feet just swingin' there over the floor like that." And that's how Lela's diminutive chair was created. *Have to admit, it's much more comfortable.*

Now, Lela Freeman, you get yourself going inside here. Already their new home was an improvement over the cabin. Since the fire Lela had been most thankful for that bunk house but she was still proud of the little lean-to their hands had built straight from the surrounding woods. *Lean-to's gone, Lela, be thankful the family is whole and has a roof at all.*

A wall stretched across the bunk house's width leaving about one-third of the space for the drovers and the rest for the Freemans. Shorty and Harry spent the better part of two days making beds and chairs for both the bunk and house sides. Lela whished through the three small sleeping rooms partitioned off across the back wall. Tidying the bed in Moses and Lela's and Solomon's rooms took no time at all. With a bed and a few pegs on the wall for hanging clothes there wasn't much that could be done. Sarah wouldn't leave her crib for a while but she would have the room between theirs and Solomon's when she was old enough.

It only took minutes, but the tightly tied bundle of broom sage cleared most of the saw dust from the small living area that remained at the end of the building. Pete had insisted that a counter and cupboards be added in a corner and a space reserved for a wood burning cook stove.

Lela couldn't imagine such luxury after cooking for nearly five years over an open fire or in a fireplace, but she didn't argue with Pete's suggestion. She was just delighted to have windows cut in on two sides. Still gaping holes, she hoped glass would be in before the nights got much cooler.

Even before more construction Lela surveyed the way the space was divided, things still weren't quite as she would have them. *It just needs some touches to make it a home* she thought. She lit an oil lamp, opened a small door in the back of Sarah's
room, and went into the narrow storage closet that was left between the bunk room and house. She came out carrying two bolts of fabric and humming Sweet Chariot as she checked on sleeping Sarah.

It was the faint humming that attracted him to the place, but when the humming turned to song, Josiah Dukes stopped his horse still. In a flash of memory he was taken to a scene from his childhood. He saw his mother stirring the wash pot and singing the very same song. That sweet picture didn't last long then or now and he shook the vision from his mind.

"Greetings to the fire," he called to announce himself. "Greetings to the fire."

Lela was startled but unafraid. All the same, she set down the fabric and stood in the open door with her hidden hand on the loaded shotgun. "Sir . . ." Lela said, leaving a question to be answered.

The portly man's velvet baritone flowed to her ear. "Madam, you are not the lady of this house, surely."

"Yes, sir. I am the lady of this house. What brings you to this place?" Lela asked trying not to betray her hope that Moses would come in from the field sooner than usual.

Removing his fancy but well-worn felt hat, he nodded formally and said, "This is a place distant from all civilization, Madam. I would take it as a great favor if I could step down and stretch my old legs and this poor steed is in need of a cooling drink."

Unable to think of a reason not to allow the man and horse to refresh and continue on, Lela nodded silently. She also knew that she was vulnerable and didn't want to risk angering a stranger whose purpose she did not know.

The man lumbered off the horse and the animal breathed deeply and sighed as though glad to be rid of his burden for even a short time. The felt hat was hung on the saddle horn. The gentleman brushed the road's dust from the faded gold brocade vest and offered introduction. "My name is Josiah Dukes, ma'am and I'm most delighted to discover a home of such obvious warmth and beauty." He bowed ceremoniously, at least as much as he could bow considering the size of his girth.

"This is the Moses Freeman farm, sir, and I am Lela Freeman." Lela didn't move from the doorway and her eyes locked onto him as he drank a dipper of water then dipped a red silky handkerchief to wash and cool his face.

"Where are you destined, Mr. Dukes?" Lela asked, hoping to learn that he had no time for more than a quick drink of water.

"Well, isn't that the question, ma'am. Isn't that the question for us all?" Dukes brushed what travel debris he could off his swallow tail coat and turned toward his horse. *Strange man* thought Lela, relieved that he was going after just a refreshing drink. *Looks like he's almost as wide as he is tall* Lela almost giggled at the rolly poly image of a big, black ball of human flesh.

To Lela's disappointment he just reached into his saddlebag and turned back to her. She knew if he saw her discomfort, things might go worse for her if he meant harm so she stepped just outside the doorway. "I was hoping, ma'am, that your husband – Moses you said – would be here to see what I have to solicit." He approached her but kept a decent distance.

He was either trustworthy after all or skilled at deception. She just wasn't sure which yet. What she did know was that the back of her neck still prickled. *I do wish Shorty and Harry would get back from town. Having even them here would make me feel better.*

The whole time Lela glanced at the pages of the small catalog he handed her, she was aware of his distance and demeanor. And the whole time he continued a rhythmic stream of miscellaneous information about some of the items that might be of particular interest to the Freemans. The pages revealed all manner of tools, plows, and other farming implements – things that would make Moses' work much easier.

Handing the catalog back after a cursory look Lela said, "True, these things look interesting and they might make my husband's work go better. But, I can't make choices for him and I know you must have other calls to make."

"Well, madam," Dukes said quietly, "I am a man of his own time cumbered by no timetable. It is my privilege to traverse this wild and beauteous country and offer its fine inhabitants the opport to improve their lot with conveniencing equipment."

Lela looked at the man with his broad smile and big words. *My, but doesn't he talk mightily. I'd just bet he thinks I don't understand a thing he says or realize that most of what he says is pure nonsense.* Just before Lela's pride could speak and chance angering the stranger, Sarah's cry notified anyone within hearing that she was awake, hungry, and demanding attention. "You may loosen the cinch on your horse, Mr. Dukes, and have another dipper of water." She gestured directly at the cook-fire log farthest from the house and turned as she said, "My husband will be back momentarily and will see you there the moment he does."

Sure enough, Moses soon arrived with two newly felled trees to be chopped for firewood. The instant he saw the strange figure at the fire, he started to leave the mules still harnessed so he could investigate. Lela, reentering the yard with Sarah on her hip, relaxed when she saw her husband approaching. More loudly than necessary, she called out, "Moses! I thought you'd be here about now." Regaining herself she added, "Unhitch the mules and I'll have you a cup of coffee."

Steaming cup of coffee in one hand and his daughter's small hand in the other, Moses heard introductions. Josiah Dukes might have been an impressive figure with a silver tongue to some, but Moses didn't take easily to new people and his cool welcome was no surprise to Lela.

It quickly became clear that Lela hadn't offered and likely wouldn't offer coffee to him as she had her husband. That also meant a hot meal and warm camp
site wouldn't be forthcoming either, so Dukes moved to business. "Mr. Freeman, my good man, you have done superlative work on this domicility. Surely, you've been here since before the war's end. May I ask where you came from?"

The man used big words, alright, but the tone seemed friendly even if Moses didn't know exactly everything he'd said. "No, sir, just these last four years. Ain't got the papers clear yet."

"Only four years, and such work has been done. I am overwhelmed and just you and your lovely wife here for the laborers. I say with utmost condor that you have wrung miracles here." The man stood and dramatically turned a full circle reviewing all within his sight. "I cannot comprehend how you have manustructed such an exceptional home in such a short time."

"Not just the two of us, Mr. Dukes. We been mighty lucky with a son who work way past his years. We got a few friends, too. Oh, it ain't been so easy at times. No sir. But we been mighty blessed I'd say."

Dukes could see that these were plain, fine people. Hard to mark. Resuming his seat on the log he withdrew the catalog from his inside coat pocket. "I can only imagine what you could do here with a few conveniences. Permit me to show you some tools and implementations that would relieve your burden significantly."

In the early falling twilight, the booklet had to be angled just so to see by the firelight. The book was

filled with drawings of farm tools large and small, some Moses had never seen. Dukes moved nearer the couple and spewed a constant stream of names, sizes, and attributes of each item available for sale. Moses could read, not nearly as well as Lela and Solomon, but he could tell from most of the pictures what the implement was designed to do. Moses could hardly keep up and just wanted to study the document in quiet. Finally, he looked up in frustration.

"Mr. Dukes, sir, I ain't mean no disrespect, but I got to have some time and breathing space to look at this here book of yours."

The big man stopped short. This wasn't an educated man and his wife had spoken very few words since he had arrived so she was hard to measure. But these weren't ordinary slaves. It would take finesse to make sales to these two. "Why, of course, Mr. Freeman. It's just that I get so enthusable about these apparitions and can see them making your life better, that I get too bold." He put his hat back on and moved slowly toward his horse. "Let me just take a moment to check on my old horse there and you just call out if you have questions." He glanced back seeing the two figures huddled over the booklet and smiled smugly.

"Moses," Lela whispered, "it's getting late and Shorty and Harry will be back from town any time."

"Uh-huh," Moses grunted, engrossed in the pictures. "Moses!" She tugged his jacket sleeve. "We Have to decide. It's almost supper time. Is this man to stay to eat? If he eats we'll be bound to let him stay the night."

"Mmm? Ah, you right, Lela." Closing the book, Moses looked toward Dukes. "Don't 'pear to be a bad sort I reckon. Got enough supper?"

"Yes, of course. But that's not what worries me. I won't have a total stranger come into our house. We couldn't dare put him in the bunk house with Shorty and Harry."

"No, you right about that. They just now actin' like they might be acceptin' bein' here," he observed. "No need stirring' 'em back up now."

"So?" Lela asked urgently.

"Reckon maybe we have him stay and offer him to bed down in the barn?"

"Are you thinking of buying from him?"

Flipping the pages of the book again, Moses pondered, "Don't know, Lela. Just don't know. Some of these shore look in'resting."

"Alright. You do the inviting. I'll finish supper and we can look at the book later in the house. I'd like us to study the pictures and talk without him," Lela's eyes darted toward the bulky figure, "hovering and pushing."

Dukes seemed grateful for supper and amenable to the barn's shelter. Having discovered entertainment in New Troy, Shorty and Harry dragged in sometime during the early morning hours and would face a day of misery trying to work. Moses and Lela poured over the booklet and Moses settled on the one piece of equipment he thought might appreciably improve his farming practices if they could haggle him enough.

The next morning they were already at the fire when the two hands stumbled from the bunk room. They shaded their eyes and rubbed their faces and heads as they tried to rub off the blurry night. Even coffee and biscuits were hard for them to manage. About the time they were ready to start hammering to build the tables they needed, which wasn't likely to make them feel any better, Mr. Dukes ambled to the water barrel and tried to wake himself up with some measure of dignity. They looked at each other, shrugged, and without a word turned in tandem back toward their room. Apparently they'd brought some of their entertainment with them from town because they got drunk. They weren't loud or rude. They simply stayed quietly drunk until the whiskey ran out after three days. Eventually, they emerged from the bunk room, went to the river to wash, and went straight to work as though they'd not missed a beat.

Josiah Dukes wasn't accustomed to early rising but knew he'd better make the effort to be courteous. Throwing cold water on his face and neck he muttered to himself. "Days like this I wonder what in thunder I'm doing. Shoulda stayed in Savannah where 'least there weren't miles between every patsy."

Dukes sat on a log with a cup of steaming coffee in his hands hoping that they could do business promptly. He had his doubts that this stop would be profitable anyway, so he was ready to move on. Moses looked at the still drowsy man hoping that they could talk their business and get Josiah Dukes on his way because he had lots to do and he'd already lost some daylight. Having poured their coffee Lela stood between them and lost the battle with her impatience. "Mr. Dukes, where do you think you will travel from here?"

With much throat clearing the man replied. "I don't precisioned have a destination, Mrs. Freeman. Perhaps you could direct me to some of your neighbors." Laughing quietly Lela told him that there were no neighbors. "In that case, my day will include a very long ride, so we might need to discuss what you good people would like from my little catalog there."

After a very brief negotiation, a price of fifteen dollars was settled on for a mule drawn plow with four feet instead of just one. It also had a steel seat on it so the driver's weight would allow for deeper plowing, a real help when breaking ground, new or old. A body would also be able to hold out to plow longer. "With two mules, Mr. Dukes, I foresee to hold out long enough to use them both in a day."

"Well, isn't that fine thinking, Mr. Freeman? That certainly does increase your ability to accomplish more by yourself," praised Dukes. "I'd not thought of it just like that," although he had certainly thought of it. That very point was one of his strongest selling points but this time he hadn't needed to use it.

Having already discussed their limits, Lela and Moses felt it was a fair deal, especially the way prices were going up since things settled down from the war. They handed the man a few coins from the metal box under Solomon's bed. That left only one coin. Two dollars. The Freemans knew that they needn't fret about taking the money because Solomon didn't consider the money in the box his. He put away whatever cash he could because they didn't have the chance for much cash and he knew to take advantage when there was some.

One more trip to the water barrel to refill his canteen and Mr. Dukes mounted his horse which let out a long sigh. Hat in hand and with a grandly sweeping gesture akin to a bow, he reminded Moses and Lela, "Now don' forget. It will take at least ten weeks to have delivery of your new equipment, so don't become impatient. I feel confidential that a shop man in New Troy will hold it until you make a trip to town. You'll pay him the balance and he'll send that on to my company for me."

"We'll look for it Mr. Dukes. New Troy ain't so big. We find for it sure," Moses called after the man.

CHAPTER EIGHT

The crew knew they'd not have another respite like they had at Dudley so, beyond taking on their routine shifts riding herd, they took their ease to store up for the hardest part of the drive. Solomon knew he wasn't welcomed like Pete but he did have free range on the farm often watching and questioning people as they used a tool or machine he wasn't familiar with. Most were willing enough to explain things to him, though some were a little grudging with their time. He ended his ramblings and accepted a couple of biscuits from Mrs. Dudley before wandering toward the woods north of the house. He still bore the unfamiliar burden of his responsibilities but walked with a lighter step than the day before.

Especially fascinated with its machines and innovations Solomon explored the farm with a closer eye to improvements he might be able to duplicate at home. He paused in the shade of a barn shed and was examining a small, hand driven grist mill when he felt her presence. He turned to face her.

"Hello, Sallie Mae."

"Hello, Mr. . . . er . . . Solomon. What are you doing in this dreary old place?" she inquired.

His interest and excitement radiated. "I was tryin' to figure out how I could make one of these. Sure would save us a heap of time and money could we grind our own grits and cornmeal."

"Y'all don't have one of these?" Sallie Mae asked with some surprise. A little embarrassed, Solomon admitted they had very few of the implements and machines he'd seen at Dudley. "Oh. I guess   I just thought . . . well, this the only place I ever lived. I reckon I thought ever'body just had what I see here."

"That's like me before we left Hunter's Run." Solomon explained. "But these last few years I been more places and seen more sights than I can hardly remember. And Mr. Pete tells me of things I just can't even picture in my mind."

"Must be excitin' to see such things," the girl observed dreamily. Sharing Solomon's biscuits, the two moved toward the woods as though they moved of one mind, spilling words onto each other with every step. The more animated their discussion, the faster they walked until finally they stopped talking and scampered randomly through the deep woods behaving exactly like the children they still were.

Finally, when they reached a little pond, they flopped at its edge and lapped the cool water between gasping for breath. Sallie Mae gave Solomon a quick sideways glance, started to grin, and heaved a hand full of water at him. Shocked for a moment, Solomon splashed right back at her as he moved knee deep into the pond. Not one to be bested, Sallie Mae moved a little deeper as her wind mill arms soaked Solomon until he collapsed trying to catch his breath.

As soon as she saw that she had won the contest, Sallie Mae also fell backwards into the water and together they laughed uncontrollably. Breathless,
Solomon sat perfectly still and stared at this amazing girl. His friend. "My friend," he whispered. "Sallie Mae, you are my only friend."

"Oh, stuff-stuff. What about that Mr. Pete you talk about and all the men on the drive? You got lots of friends, Solomon," she asserted.

"No. That's not what I mean." He had trouble knowing precisely what he did mean. "**My** friend . . . my age . . . you are the only friend I've got that's truly **my** friend."

They stood, rinsed the pond sediment from themselves, and moved toward the bank. "Well, Solomon Freeman," Sallie Mae said thoughtfully. Her face wrinkled in thought. "You must be my only friend, too."

"That's hard to believe with all the folks around here."

"You right, they's lots of 'em sure and I reckon I know 'em all – dark and light." Her face changed as this awareness came clear to her. "But ain't such a thing as bein' friends with white ones, even them I knowed all my life. Ain't lots of younguns here. Most went their way after 'mancipation. And the rest are way older."

"Well, then, looks like we got to keep bein' friends if we the only ones we got!" Solomon said firmly. He looked upward through the trees where the sun told him it was time to get back to check the animals and eat supper. As Sallie Mae walked away Solomon admired the slender muscular figure to which her still wet shift clung.

CHAPTER NINE

Driving cattle consisted of long, exhausting days in weather that was too hot, too cold, too wet, or too dry. There was little amusement to be found and even less time in which to enjoy it should it be found. A last smoke or chew after supper found the drovers bedding down because, even if they didn't have night watch, the next day began well before daylight.

Despite the grueling toil, Solomon, like the other men, found pleasure in the work itself. Being in the open air, observing the gifts of nature, and cracking a joke once in a while were the benefits. Angus, although relatively new to the country, was one of the more experienced drovers. As was his habit, he waxed philosophical as he and Solomon moved a few more cows toward the main herd. "'Tis a way of life, me boyo, to be loved or to be hated. There'll be wee little in between. Should a man love it he can hardly bear the wait for the next drive."

"Yes sir, I reckon that's so."

"'Tis true, indeed. I'll nay say I'm knowing of such as cattle drives in the heathered hills, it was sheep for me, nay the heurry coos. But the self-same rule applies to most any work, light or hard. Aye, I've seen wi' me own eyes strapping men locked into work they despised." Puzzled, Solomon slowed Swamp Foot to match Angus' slowed tempo and saw a marble-faced man looking at visions of his past. Just before he stopped altogether, Angus' blinked hard and his face softened. "Me own Da I still see. Never was there a man who loved more the purity of a clear day and the progress of a growing thing. But, he came home every day from the depths of hell black with coal dust, wearier and weaker than the day before – until that last day when he was so weak he couldn't pull himself from his bed. Lasted only three days more, he did."

"I'm sorry, Mr. Angus. I didn't know."

The man sighed and continued, his voice still aching, "Just a lad I was and near broke me Mam's heart when I determined to leave and seek other fortunes. But, then she wouldna want the miner's life for her only son. Aye, there be nay choice betimes." The two rode in silence until they merged with the herd.

By the time they moved south again the gloomy mood was broken and Solomon felt free to talk again.

"Were you married in Scotland?"

"Married?" Angus groaned softly. "From where does that question come, me boyo?"

"Nowhere, I guess." Solomon fumbled for an explanation but he didn't have one.

"Nay, lad, not married." Angus' horse stopped and the man's eyes stared into the woods as though to another world. Solomon tried to see what his friend saw. "No, not married, but wished to be. Indeed, I so longed to be."

"Why didn't you . . . ?

"Ah, her name was Kaye. Sweet, sweet Kaye of the auburn hair and freckles sprinkled across her nose with the bonniest laugh that rang through the forest."

"She sounds nice," Solomon said wistfully.

"Nice? Ach, nice canna tell it. We were so in tuned with one another but . . . but alas . . . it was no good." Solomon just couldn't ask anything more. He almost didn't want to hear what must come next. "Me Da died, I had now a widowed mother to support and did so by sending money to her for the short time she lived after I left home. But I had to leave home. There was no work to be had at home and I had no prospects to offer to Kaye. Her father wouldna hear of it; wouldna even meet with me." Angus shook his head slowly and moved his horse forward.

Swamp Foot followed and Solomon tried to find words that would ease the pain Angus clearly felt after what must be many years now. "Do you know what happened to Kaye?" he whispered.

"I saw her a last moment before I sailed to America with a promise that I would try to come back with enough success to prove myself to her Da." Angus exhaled long and slowly. "But we both knew that was just a dream. We knew we loved one another but that we could not be together. There canna be harder pain."

"I'm sorry Mr. Angus. You and Miss Kaye didn't deserve that. You deserved to be together."

"Aye, Solomon, aye we did. We promised our hope to eternity. That's what we both must trust on."

The men rode and worked for a long time each with his own thoughts before Solomon spoke again. He found Angus a wise and thoughtful man and felt a deep kinship with him. Maybe Angus felt some of the darknesses that he felt. That would be something to ask him someday. Finally, not wanting to miss his

opportunity, Solomon asked quietly, "Mr. Angus, did you and your Papa ever disagree when you were a boy?" Solomon asked quietly.

"Oh, must be that's a rule, me boy. Every son must pull from his father and every father must push at his son. But in the main I ken me Da and meself more admired than detested one another." Angus stopped, hoping the boy felt he could confide his worries.

"I guess so. Just my Papa and me ain't cut from the same cloth atall. No sir, I love him, I do. And I think we got respect but we just too different. I know it gets mighty hard out here but I can't know of a single thing I druther do than be out among the woods and critters."

"Aye, lad, 'tis a fine world surrounds us. Me," he said looking upward through the treetops, "I note the clouds. Clouds have moods, they do. They have music and dance of their own."

"For pure beauty it must be the sunrises and sunsets that grab my spirit. Ain't no man can make such a picture. Just God can paint that."

"Ah, right you are, lad, so right you are."

Solomon brightened as he took another look at the two furry beasts flying round and round the herd. "S'pose critters in their own places is really my first choice though. And I found me another kind of critter to admire. I believe I could watch them dogs work all the day long."

"I see your point." Still in his Highlands reverie, Angus continued. "They bring to mind the breeds that herd the sheep in the Highlands. Different from these in looks, but the work and their skills are the same. A wondrous thing 'tis, to watch not-so-very-large dogs working with a solitary man to bring sheep to shearing." Well into fall, it was still warm on horseback and Angus wiped his face and neck with a faded red bandana.

"They do this same thing with the sheep, do they, Angus? The running round and round to keep the herd in a bunch?"

"Aye," Angus replied. "Mind, there are differences. There's some less barking among the sheep as they'd be of a more skittish character than cattle, but the circling and nipping to bring strays back into the fold is the same." Dropping the reins and demonstrating with his hands, Angus went on. "Some of them do this just by knowing it's their job to do. But most times it grows into a true team, man and dog looking each to the other for the next step to take."

"How do you mean?" Solomon was spellbound.

"Never done myself, mind, but the gentleman I tended for as a lad was a master. A good man and a good dog, eyes each on the other, are like a fine tuned dance step. And make it so simple to watching eyes. Some men use whistle commands while others use hand motions. Either way they get it done like a grand dance set."

"Don't know how it'd possibly happen, but surely it'd be a lucky thing to have one for my own," the boy said wistfully.

Offering neither encouragement nor discouragement, Angus simply answered, "'Twould, indeed." Solomon didn't have to tell anyone he'd fallen for those dogs. He didn't disturb them while they were at work and after, from a fair distance, they'd begged bits for supper from all the men. But, the two furry beasts knew they had a friend in the boy and most mornings the trio could be found knotted together warming each other.

As much as Solomon would love to take the dogs from the main herd, he knew they were where they should be because they covered the work of three or four men. Neither cow hunter had time to daydream about dogs they would never own because two full grown cows came lumbering out of the scrub almost colliding with the riders. Immediately, the men shifted into action, whips loosely in hand.

The animals were skittish and one of them might have qualified as mean. The two men moved to guide them toward Cookie's path. These cows demanded plenty of space or they would just bolt into the deep woods never to be seen again, so Solomon and Angus moved slowly, swinging doubled up whips in cadence with their low chucking and whistles. As soon as the dogs saw new meat approaching, they moved into an instinctive tandem.

Muscular and steady if not fast, Hardtack increased his pace slightly and moved in a continual semi-circle monitoring the entire herd. Scar trusted Hardtack to keep the cattle moving and loped toward the approaching figures. Lean, alert, and fast but calm, Scar moved in behind the cows, barking quietly and nipping to turn them toward the center of the herd. Scar knew these were not beasts to be charged or rushed; he moved around them with smooth confidence.

The least friendly of the old cows wheeled around to challenge the nuisance at her heels only to get a sharp nip on the nose. The old girl gave up the frontal challenge and moved on docilely. The great slice in Scar's side shone black where the hair had never grown back after his near death experience with a wild boar's tusks as a pup. But Scar was fearless and unrelenting, intent on getting those cows exactly where he wanted them. Bouncing from side to side giving fair attention to each cow, Scar was in a rhythm that he could sustain for hours. Suddenly, the wild old gal threw her weight forward and violently kicked backward with both feet. One hoof connected with head while the other caught belly and Scar flew up and around until he landed hard about eight feet away.

Solomon immediately wheeled Swamp Foot toward the thicket where he saw the wiry dog disappear dreading what he expected to find. He launched off Swampy and plowed into the thicket. There wasn't even much blood – just a cut on top of an already swelling forehead. Except for a nearly imperceptible rise and fall of breathing, the dog was stone still. Scar wasn't dead. Yet.

As he'd seen Pete and Cookie do so often, Solomon methodically rubbed his hands all over the dog's motionless body to assess the damage. When Solomon pressed lightly on Scar's side a weak groan alerted the boy to internal damage. However, unlike Pete, he knew little about exactly what it was he felt as he completed the examination. Slowly, carefully Solomon half cradled, half pulled the dog into the clear. The valiant cur tried to rise only to fall back into the dirt, but not flat out this time. The blinking eyes in his wobbly head tried to steady their vision.

"Hold, boy," Solomon soothed as he gently rubbed his head. "Come on, Scar, you've seen worse than an old cow kicking you." The boy hated even thinking of what might happen next. He talked to encourage the dog. He listened to encourage himself.

Soon Scar looked directly at Solomon, eyes clear and straight, and lapped the canteen water from the boy's palm continuing to lick the salty hand as if to thank Solomon for his caring. Starting at his head, Scar breathed in and flexed his whole body clear to his tail. Then he sat up, trembled a bit, and stood on all fours. "Don't go too fast, boy. I can carry you back to the camp and Mr. Cookie will fix you right up." Scar looked at Solomon again, narrowed his eyes in concentration, and started to walk in the direction of the herd. Solomon led Swamp Foot closely behind the dog and watched him take step after step, testing every part of his body to shake off the thumping from the cow.

Pausing to rest occasionally and stretch some more, the trek took considerable time. But Scar walked right into camp, past the night fire, and unswervingly to the chuck wagon where he seemed to know both the food and treatment he needed were to be found. Hardtack left his post long enough to see that his partner was alive and to smell the scent of injury well enough to know he didn't want to get very close. Soon he returned to duty.

With a little coaching from Cookie, Solomon did what he could to ease the dog. He was breathing hard, head lolling, little droplets still oozing from the head wound. Scar winced as Angus helped wrap around the old scar on the dog's chest tightly hoping to repair the ribs Solomon was almost sure had been cracked or broken. They sponged clean and anointed the head wound. As Cookie worked over the dog, Solomon talked to him as though it was the most natural thing in the world and the dog understood every word. "Hold, old boy. I know this gotta hurt." No whimpering was heard through incredible pain; there was just an occasional flinch.

"I swear," Solomon would relate at the supper fire, "it was like every time he looked at me he was talking' right to me. 'No boy gonna carry me to no camp. If I can't walk myself, it's time for me to stay here and die.'" The boy went on with admiration shared by most of the company, "Didn't whimper, not once, but I know he's hurt bad."

"Don't see what all the fuss and bother be about," grumbled George, who was by nature sullen and rarely spoke. "Act like that mangy cur was a top hand or somethin'."

Cowboys put great stock in men, horses and dogs who worked hard, knew their craft, and didn't whine and linger over hurt. They also knew that sometimes those who didn't own up to their injuries, didn't make it for long. And they didn't much care for George's remarks. Charlie had to weigh in, pointing his nubby arm right at the new man. "George, you're still pretty new to this work and you ain't seen much of the life. Don't go sellin' a good dog short. No, sir, a real good dog can equal half a dozen men. You don't want longer watch shifts, you'll start hoping right along with the rest of us that that dog comes through this no worse for wear."

"Time for my watch anyway," George groused. He was still muttering as he left the fire. "Ain't no mutt worth all that much. Think them dogs could do the drive right by theirselves." The men just shook their heads in wonder at a man in such a mood of constant gloom and complaint.

After just two days of riding with Cookie on the seat of the chuck wagon – and wanting to get back on the ground every minute of it – Scar rejoined Hardtack. They touched noses timidly and Hardtack inspected Scar's wound suspiciously, eyes betraying his recognition of the still evident smell of blood. They circled each other a few times before Scar stood firm and gave a great shake. Within minutes the two dogs were working their routine as though they'd never missed a beat.

Scar sometimes appeared disoriented and it took him a few days to regain his full steadiness and stamina. Hardtack sensed Scar's condition and picked up his pace to cover some of Scar's space around the herd. The wounded dog would not look the same, though, as his head bore a half-moon shaped half healed scar where the hoof had engraved the skin and the hair might never grow back. Now Scar's name was doubly fitting.

It seemed that, heat or cold and tongues hanging, both dogs could work all day long. Just pause the drive for anything, though, and they found the nearest shade available. They could fall into full sleep and come to alert faster than Solomon thought possible.

Predictably, the bigger the herd got the more the pace slowed. Still they had reached the prairie in good time. Slim remarked about it over a final cup of hot coffee. "Near 'bout gone too smooth us getting' this far so fast. Reckon the boss's plan works and the good luck stays with us." His observation wasn't directed at anyone in particular and he got no specific reply, just a chorus of agreeable grunts and head nods.

Since they'd bedded down on the north side of the broad, flat stretch of random trails through thick swamp and grassy knolls, they broke camp well before daylight – even earlier than usual. A couple of the new hands grumbled, as they'd done about most everything so far, that, "Ain't no need spending' so many hours in the saddle you 'bout caint stand up straight and ain't got 'enough feelin' in you're a-uh- backside to know it's still there."

Solomon offered some orientation for the new men. "Nobody looks forward to this ride, but you'll soon see crossing the prairie in one day is the only way to do it." He reminded them that the eastern side of the prairie was more a lake except in severe drought and urged vigilance in keeping the herd to the far western side. There would be enough to watch out for without cows trying to swim all the way to solid ground.

Manuel who, though warm and friendly to those he knew, still wasn't very talkative in the larger company, explained cryptically, "*Sí, Señors,* you do not know what *Senor Dios* keep in this place." The little man mounted his horse and crossed himself thrice as though to ward off an evil spell.

To emphasize the dangers, Solomon repeated for those present the instructions he'd given the night before. "It'll be next to impossible to keep the herd bunched like usual so we got to ride 'em loose. Don't lose sight or control of 'em, but don't ride 'em too close either. Main thing is to keep 'em on firm ground. Watch for that." Solomon paused, shook his head matter of factly, and made his final comment. "Ain't no explainin' it – but you see for yourselves." They moved out but it was obvious the complainers thought the whole bunch of them were mad, as though they thought the prairie was somehow hexed or haunted.

Just as Solomon predicted, the cows, wagon, and men on horseback had to pick the best paths they could through the muddled bog and around genuine bodies of water. At least the terrain was flat so they could keep in sight of each other, but that might have been the only good point of it. With Manuel scouting, Cookie and the wagon tried to work the maze without leaving firm ground. That wasn't always possible, but they managed pretty well. Just as soon as they reached the south side and solid ground, they set up camp on a little hill overlooking the prairie.

Cookie gazed across its expanse and said, "Looks so beautiful and calm from up here and no tellin' what murderous creatures lurk there." Manuel crossed himself twice and helped Cookie set last night's beans to heating and the coffee to boiling. They knew it would be a late night and wanted hot food and hotter coffee ready.

The men managed pretty well keeping the cows bunched. Not all together, but in smallish groups with a man roughly in control. Scar and Hardtack alternated between animated curiosity and bafflement in this foreign terrain as they raced from group to group wanting desperately to reform the herd as they knew it was supposed to be.

By about half way across Solomon made rounds and especially wanted to hear from the morning's whiners. "Okay, Boss. You right about this place," one of them admitted. "I just want to get on across 'fore dark. I seed snakes and big lizards and rustlin' grass I didn't want to know what was doin' the rustlin'."

"I know exactly what you mean. Just keep your eyes open and keep 'em movin'," Solomon encouraged.

"You got it. I ain't lookin' to still be out here when the haints come stirring'."

Solomon couldn't help chuckling and reassured the men that the day was going remarkably well and he didn't anticipate any problems from this point on.

About half the herd had regrouped between the last of the marsh and the chuck wagon but it was nearly sunset and Slim feared for anything left on the prairie once night came. He stood in his stirrups and tried to calculate how far away the stragglers were. Tight lips showed he wasn't sure but, with luck he thought they'd make it before last light.

He gestured for two other men who had already made it to the haven of firm ground and they headed back toward the bog to help things along. Farther east than he'd expected to, he saw a couple of cows milling and lowing and a single rider flailing his arms wildly. Slim headed that way as fast as he could navigate the labyrinth and his sharp whistle brought the other two cow hunters in the same direction. Before they reached the spot, they lost sight of the man but could still hear him shrieking. By the time the men reached their comrade they could only see the horse's ears and the man from chest up, his arms still flailing.

George pulled his horse up with a jerk, just before stepping into the slush himself. "Godamighty!" he said with a shudder. "Can't hardly tell a difference 'tween the sand and this muddy part." As reassuringly as he could he encouraged Big Jim. "We're here Jim, don't fight it. You struggle more, you sink more."

"Can't say I'm terrible sorry to see you men," Big Jim said in that dry, wry humor of his.

"Hold, Jim," shouted Slim. It didn't take much to know they had to act quickly. Slim spat commands matching the speed of his lariat swung over his head. Slim's rope looped Big Jim and was double wrapped around his oversized saddle horn. "Alright," Slim ordered, "we got to move him and to pull 'em out the short side."

George had seen quicksand before and knew this was a deep one. The horse was already lost and saving Big Jim might be the longest shot he'd seen in a long time, his rope also lassoed Big Jim.

The quicksand appeared to overpower Big Jim's slight frame. He was trying to pull himself away from the saddle but there was some sort of vacuum established that made it almost impossible. George's horse pulled in tandem with Slim as gently and continuously as possible and it seemed to be working a little then Jim lurched slightly forward then stopped.

The thick, grainy mud's hands pulled Big Jim's legs down to Hades with the sinners of the world. On the surface it was hard to tell where the sandy mound stopped and the killing mud started. "Near there, boys," Slim encouraged wishing his friend wasn't quite so deep. "You hold on there Big Jim. May not feel like it but you're moving. You get free of the horse and we can drag you right on out of there.""Jim!" Slim ordered. "You got to let that horse go!" "Caint do it, Slim," Jim's shaking voice replied.

"Poor old boy so afeared he just dug himself right in. Hate losing old thing. Good horse."

"He's pullin' you right under with him," one of the others shouted.

"I caint pull free," the sinking man called. "Too much gone to move anything." A momentary shudder suggested Big Jim was in emotional collapse.

The more hope the men lost, the harder they tugged. The harder they tugged, the harder the demon hands pulled from below, but they couldn't give up on Jim.

Solomon arrived from the camp site in time to see the final scene play out. The men called words of encouragement to him, "Jim, hold on. Rest easy, boy." All the while, they looked at their doomed comrade.

Jim could barely speak. "You git word to my missus and I thank you for tryin'." Then, his face turned flat up to the sky and the most peaceful look came over him. "Look at that sunset, boys. Thank you for that, Lord. Ain't nothin' perttier than sunset in the scrub."

Hats in hands, they just stared into the gray muck, each man saying his own benediction for their friend. Even the most hardened of them prayed. Slowly, disheartened they turned toward camp, soon encountering a tiny spot of open water. It was just a muddy little pond, but they fell into it writhing like men possessed, clawing to get the killer mud from their clothes and bodies.

Well after dark, the men stumbled into camp where men were at the ready to tend their mounts. They collapsed at the fire, took offered plates, and methodically ate whatever was on those plates. The story was told only once that night, but would be told quietly over and over from every angle before the end of the drive, and the location of the quicksand was etched into the mental maps of every man there.

Solomon had stayed on a while after the others left the deathly site, and only came to camp after all was quiet. He unrolled his blanket at a distance from the camp where Scar and Hardtack had waited up to comfort him.

CHAPTER TEN

Moving through Levy County toward Way Key might have been the easiest stretch of the whole drive – at least physically. Except maybe that the flies were even worse than Solomon remembered and the sugar sand was like dry quicksand. It was quiet, though, with little beyond necessary conversation. Extra words somehow seemed loud and harsh – almost disrespectful. Despite the discomfort, they made fair time and camped in the familiar location near the last fresh water source before crossing over to Way Key.

The business patterns were reasonably well established – Solomon, Slim, and Manuel rode to the island for a day and night to scout prospective buyers. These weren't ships that ran on precise schedules so the men could never be sure how many would be in port, where they might be headed, or which ones might already be contracted. More than last year, Solomon hoped that they would see a familiar captain's face or two. They'd established relationships with a few of the Cuban captains and the steamships going west across the Gulf of Mexico. Pete's operation quickly earned a reputation for high quality animals and fair dealing and the greenhorn trail boss didn't want to negotiate fresh. He knew he needed the strength of Pete's reputation to lean on.

As soon as they left the herd for the key, Solomon's palms started to sweat and beads popped out across his forehead. Manuel noticed the boss's rigid features and attempted to lighten the mood.

"Señor Trail Boss. We are here! There is no worry to be so serious." Manuel didn't see much change in Solomon's demeanor, so he started singing, urging Solomon to join in as it was a song he knew well.

"Manuel, you may as well just sing in the wind today," said Slim, treading the tightrope between mood-lightening humor and making fun. "Mr. Freeman has a lot on his mind, being boss and all. You know they's lots of difference ridin' in our saddles as hands and ridin' in the boss's saddle."

"Sí, Señor Slim," agreed Manuel. "I sing anyway, you don't mind." They both knew there were dark clouds in Solomon's mind and the clouds weren't all about the sales.

The tricky crossing to the island of Way Key at low tide was flawless and the men bedded down in their customary place under palm trees a ways from the docks. Others had found their spot, too, but there was ample space open for three more men and horses.

Strolling along the docks, they scouted the ships as they headed toward a restaurant. "Well, I know this one thing," vowed Slim unexpectedly. Manuel and Solomon looked at Slim and each other startled. "We goin' to the restaurant we want to and we ALL gon' eat supper together." "Sí, Señor. If not all, then not one," Manuel agreed.

"Solomon must be respected as our boss."

"Yup," nodded Slim. "Yessir, we're goin' right to the place didn't like his looks that first year. We been back there?" The tilt of Manuel's head agreed not and the decision was made before Solomon could say he didn't care as long as he got something to eat. He just didn't want anything to go wrong with the business dealings. "Yessir, from T-bone to apple pie, that's right where we ALL eat."

Eat they did, too. The proprietor wasn't keen on the trio – burly white, swarthy Spaniard, and peach-fuzz colored. But the approach that Slim took left him little choice. They had a prime table and treated themselves to oysters, charred and red-running T-bones, mountains of mashed potatoes, and hot crispy-crusted apple pie.

A last walk past the ships, Solomon rubbed his belly and just smiled. "I done had 'bout the best meal I ever had in my whole life." He quickly realized what he had said and corrected, "'sides my mama's cooking, mind you."

"Sí, Solomon. *Señora Lela's cocina is very delicious*."

Slim laughed, "And it don't matter that kitchen's a stove or one pot fire. She's some cook, your mama."

"Yessir, she is," Solomon agreed. "But tonight was specially good."

"Tonight weren't beans and biscuits!" Slim said, laughing out loud. The men found their bedrolls and settled in near a low burning fire. After a short time Slim turned serious. "Solomon, I know you're still awake. You got to know me and Manuel will do everything we can to make things right tomorrow, but you're the boss on this drive."

"I know you will, Slim, and I thank you." The boy didn't sound confident.

"Sí, Amigo. We Mr. Pete's outfit but it is the boss who must make the business."

Almost inaudibly, Solomon answered. "Oh, I know that for sure, Manuel. I don't need a reminder on that."

"Guess what me and Manuel tryin' to say, Solomon, is we know you're nervous about tomorrow. But, we trust you. Pete himself can't talk Spanish to the Cubans and figure cows to coins as good as you." Wishing he knew more to say, Slim finished with, "You get a good sleep. No need worryin' on what ain't gon' be a problem."

As soon as they moved toward the pier, Solomon and his men could see that two more ships had birthed during the night, increasing the potential for sales. They didn't see even one familiar ship and didn't look forward to establishing ties with totally new captains. But, the day was young and there was work to be done. After over five hours of introductions, intense negotiations, and strangling nerves, the entire herd had tickets out of Way Key.

"I ain't afraid to say I'm glad that part's over," Solomon said, exhaling a huge breath as they mounted their horses. "Didn't do a bit of good to have Pete's good name with us 'cause none of these captains know him."

"Sí, Solomon," Manuel added. "After the first *capitan* I feared that all would turn from dealing with such a group as we." Crossing himself three times, he continued. *"Gracias, al Señor Dios* that not all men feel as he does. I believe that man had *Corazon de Diablo.*"

Slim laughed then immediately corrected the glares coming his way. "No, no, I ain't laughin' at it being funny. When you look at it from their eyes, though, you got to see the joke in it." With a keen eye for irony, Slim went on. "Three mixed breeds like us – one of 'em just a striplin' – comin' in right off the trail. Well, first you got to know it wasn't a pretty sight."

He could hardly talk through his chuckles and the other two began to see his point. "How they gonna know we even got any cows? I ain't seen many ships but sure we saw some filthy boats and tattered sailors on this trip. And sure they'd think we was just borned and could be drove right into the floor in a deal."

"But, look at some of them, Slim," Solomon remarked. "I'm not all too sure all of those ships will still be there when we get back tomorrow. They were sure a lower lot than the ones we signed with before."

Chest puffed up proudly, Manuel added, "They did not expect you to be so smart, Solomon. But they really did not expect to hear you speak such *Español*. You must have *professor muy bueno*, eh?" Slim and Solomon laughed and nodded in agreement at Manuel's compliment to himself. "Our Solomon, he did well, no, Señor Slim?"

"Our boy did well, for sure, Manuel. Pete can be real proud and them cowmen along the way better hope to know they gettin' a fine return on their beef."

Solomon, forever embarrassed by such flattery, guffawed. "I didn't do what Pete could've done. I must have wished a thousand times just this morning to have him here instead of me!"

"Well, 'tis done and done well, my Boy Boss," announced Slim, using a title that might be taken slanderously by ears beyond the trio.

There wasn't time for celebration, though. Not yet. The trio headed right back to the herd to organize the trek back across the shallows on the next morning's low tide. The herd was bigger than ever – a few over four hundred head – and the crossing would take longer. "I worry about the timing," Solomon thought out loud. "The tides go pretty fast and we can't afford to lose any cows. Can't go back on our deal neither so we got to get them all there tomorrow."

Slim agreed. "True it'll be a close thing. We'll get to camp in plenty of time to sort things, split the herd and crew, and we'll leave there before first light in the morning."

"Once tide's out just enough to start, we can get 'em moving," Solomon continued the brainstorming, "and will have to keep 'em tight and move 'em fast as we can." Both the other men knew what worried Solomon. The danger of hurrying through an outgoing tide loomed over both man and beast. The danger of not hurrying was worse.

Three days later, most of the weary drovers moved north again. A couple of the new men had broken off and stayed on Way Key doing mischief Solomon hadn't even dreamed of. Here and there a man peeled from the group as he neared the closest route to home. Most, however, stayed together to finish the work. As much as he wished to be done with the burden of being trail boss, Solomon knew That getting the cows to sea is just the first half of the job.

This time there were four wagons full to overflowing with goods from all along the Gulf coast, Cuba, and even Barbados. The seamen may have been an unsavory lot this trip but they had excellent goods. At least Solomon hoped he had judged well. He'd never been anywhere much, so he eagerly listened to suggestions from the drovers and just prayed that they had made good merchandise choices.

Again the prairie proved ominous. Just before the crossing began, the wagons were set upon by raiders. It happened so fast Solomon couldn't be sure he recognized any of them as those they'd encountered several times before – those from south of the homestead. The prairie was a little far afield for them, but greed knows few boundaries so it could've been them. Something seemed familiar about a couple of voices but it was hard to study faces while being shot at. His crew only suffered a few nicks and grazes while they dropped six of the marauders. Once things calmed, Solomon inspected the dead, but didn't recognize any of them as those who had assaulted his family years before. The certainty that there were any number of renegade bands in the region hit Solomon like a new dawn. It was logical. He just hadn't thought about it before.

Sure that their wounds weren't serious Solomon said, "That makes about enough for today. We'll bed down here and push on early tomorrow."

"Thanks, Boss," several men murmured. Charlie, rubbing the stump at the end of his elbow on his forehead nervously, observed, "Already been a long day but that last little excitement bears a rest I'd say."

"I'd say you're right, Charlie." In heightened alert, Solomon continued, "Pull the wagons in close, make sure things are tied down good, set night watchmen, get some supper, and throw it in for the night. Want to make Dudley tomorrow."

Slim nodded toward the tall slender figure moving toward a hilly spot to gaze at the sunset. "Say our Boy Boss got some things on his mind, Manuel," whispered Slim.

"Sí, Senor Slim. I think from now the prairie will always be a place of evil danger in his heart."

"True enough. He took losing Big Jim hard, like he was responsible for everything on the drive." A glint in his eye, Slim added conspiratorially, "Must be expecting something at Dudley, though, in such an all fired hurry to get there. He'd like to have got there yesterday." Slim almost whispered as he looked at Solomon in the distance. "Maybe gettin' to Dudley will give him some peace."

CHAPTER ELEVEN

As Solomon hoped, by the next twilight the wagons pulled into Dudley. At least they could go right to the place instead of bedding the herd at Camp Sink since the Dudleys had an open camp for travelers across the main road from the farm. They pulled in, greeted Cap'n Dudley, ate cold, and went to sleep. Way into fall, winter was nipping so they clustered their blankets close around the fire Cookie had built as soon as they stopped. It would be then quick work to stoke the coals and have a much needed hot breakfast. Next morning would just have to be time enough to conclude this year's dealings with the Captain. Solomon surely wanted to be well rested and straight thinking before trying to sell goods and settle up with him.

Being sure not to encroach on the Dudley's privacy or provisions, the crew had coffee and biscuits from the chuck wagon as they had every morning of the drive. Solomon stood and he, Scar, and Hardtack stretched the last of the night's kinks out of their frames. He got just a glimpse of yellow moving between the detached kitchen and the smoke house and knew – hoped – it must be atop a tall, graceful body but his glance was so quick he couldn't be sure of what or who he had seen. There was bustle at this time of day as nobody laid idle for long at Dudley.

Before the trail boss could ponder whether he had seen a person or a phantom, Captain Dudley approached. Rubbing his instantly sweaty palms on his dungarees, Solomon met the captain at the edge of their little camp. "Mornin' Cap'n Dudley, sir. Cup of coffee for you?"

Dudley took the steaming tin cup as his eyes bored right into the nervous boy. "Well," he almost sneered, "you ain't got no more cows so I reckon you must have got some money for me."

"Yes sir, I surely do." About half of their profit was in the form of gold Spanish coins stored in a small undistinguished trunk stowed in the chuck wagon. The gold was good tender in most places and would be helpful to Pete's banking venture. The rest was in paper money for easy payment to the cattlemen they owed along the trail. Solomon felt the burden of the bills stowed in the money belt around his waist. It wasn't the weight of the currency; it was the responsibility for its safety. He would be glad when it was mostly paid out.

The crew had moved on to tend horses or browse Dudley's tiny mercantile so Solomon and the captain had the dying fire to themselves. Sitting on a supply box, Solomon reached for the little notebook and stubby pencil in his pocket. It wasn't hard to see that Dudley was impatient and the trail boss didn't want to do anything to delay concluding their business.

"I hope I ain't gonna be sorry I sent them cows with you, boy," Dudley said ominously.

"I hope not, too, sir." He flipped a few pages and reviewed the notes on the page marked DUDLEY. Solomon didn't want to prolong this and irritate the captain. But it was important to him that the men they did business with knew that he had been serious and careful with their investments. "I'm not altogether sure just how Mr. Pete kept his record, Captain. But I put each herd on its own page." Turning the notebook for Captain Dudley to see, Solomon said, "Here's yours – Captain Dudley, 87 cows."

"That's the number I sent alright," agreed Dudley wondering what Solomon was up to.

"We timed it into Way Key about right and there were new ships in ready to sell out their goods and get cargo to sail out."

Solomon seemed to be checking his figures while he talked. "We figured the payouts like Mr. Pete does. After all the sales were done, the total price earned is divided by the total number in the herd. The payout is divided equally per number of cows added to the large herd with Pete's contracted percentage ciphered and taken out."

"Sounds fair," said Dudley a little surprised. "Appears you kept good records. Let's see if your figurin' is right."

"I been over it a dozen times," Solomon admitted with an anxious laugh. "Here we got your share right here." He stood just enough to hand the notebook to the captain and sat back down, restoring the pencil to his pocket and reaching for the money belt.

Solomon hadn't needed the man's wrinkled brow to tell him that the captain hadn't expected such accurate and businesslike response. Dudley's big hands fumbled with the pages and found it all noted: the amount received for the entire herd, the portion of that total for his 87 cows, and the deduction of Pete's share. The final figure was accurate and, almost to his disappointment, more than he'd expected. "I have to say, boy, you seem to have it all down." The man paused, struggling to admit the drive's success without giving Solomon too much of the credit. "Must be hard lookin' for beef to pay so good. Prices better than I expected."

"Yes sir, I guess we had some luck with it. I hope you're satisfied." The notebook was traded for a stack of cash. Solomon knew this deal wouldn't be concluded with a handshake as it would have with Pete. He knew Dudley wouldn't accept him. He also knew Dudley had been forced to improve his opinion of a novice trail boss.

As Captain Dudley stood to leave, Solomon cleared his throat. "Captain? If you have just a few minutes I'd like you to take a look at the goods we brought up."

"Anything good, boy?"

"Pretty good, I think, sir. Maybe some stock for your store?" Solomon held his breath while Dudley deliberated.

"Got any spirits? Never hurts to have a few bottles of whiskey laid back."

"Yes, sir. We got good Cuban rum. Real clear and golden it is."

"Now how do you know it's good? You a drinker now?" Dudley looked down at the boy and laughed – really laughed – for the first time with Solomon's.

"Uh, no, sir. No, sir, I ain't interested. I don't even think it smells good," the young man stammered. "But Slim and Angus and, well most of the men, they tried it and it seemed to set pretty well with them." Solomon shook his head slowly. "Must've set real well with some of 'em much as they put down."

"Alright then. A dozen bottles of rum, but careful moving it to the barn. I'll send a man that'll know just where to put it." He handed a few bills back to Solomon and added, "If you have things a lady might like or might sell good, you talk to Mrs. Mary about that."

"Thank you, Captain. I sure am glad you're satisfied with the drive this year." A yellow spot in the distance distracted Solomon. As he followed what he thought he saw he added, "Look to seein' you again next time." Captain P.B. H. Dudley grunted and got on with his day.

Solomon was relieved but still filled with nervous energy so he started a tour of the homestead to see what might be new and different on the place. A new mule, more chickens, fewer turkeys, and the kind of constant activity required to keep such a place productive was what Solomon saw. When he stepped into the little store it took a moment for his eyes to adjust to the dark. The young man bit off another little bite of the peppermint stick he'd become so fond of since Pete gave him the first one several years ago, and spied the yellow phantom again, this time moving stock. When she saw Solomon, she slipped out of sight – both surprising and disappointing.

Preoccupied, he said, "Mrs. Dudley, the Captain said I was to speak to you about the goods we brought back."

"Why, yes, Solomon. Do you think you have things I could use here?"

"I can't be full sure, ma'am, but I think so. We got wagons full if you care to look." As they walked toward the wagons, Mrs. Dudley proved more approachable than the Captain, although she explained that he really wasn't as stern as he liked to pretend. Solomon wasn't sure that applied to him though – he thought Dudley was every bit at stern with him as he meant to be.

With a couple of men to help unpack items and his notebook and pencil to record the sales, Mrs. Dudley found more of interest than either of them expected. She seemed to have tastes and uses for items Solomon would never have predicted. But then she was in charge of running a large home and farm so she would know about all manner of needs. The store would be restocked of things often hard to come by.

There were bolts of fabric, Louisiana rice, a few oranges and cigars from Cuba, and a collection of ivory, shell, and bone buttons and hair dressings. She even chose a couple of rifles and some hand guns from Texas and ammunition to match.

When Solomon opened a box filled with layers of gold and silver jewelry, Mary Dudley's eyes sparkled. "Oh, I don't think these're grand jewels, ma'am, you see that better'n me. But the gold and silver is real enough."

She gave a deep chuckle and said, "Oh, Solomon, do you know how long it's been since we've seen any niceties like this?" She picked up, inspected, tried on, and held up to gleam in the sun bracelets, rings, earrings, and pendants. "Since long before the war," she said wistfully. "And a woman's eye always rests on things of beauty." She added with an ounce of cynicism, "Even a woman in the wilderness." She turned to the boy. "Was it your eye that saw to buy these things, Solomon?"

A little embarrassed that he had been attracted by such frippery, he admitted, "Yes ma'am. I guess I was just thinkin' of things I'd sure like my Mama to have one day. They'd look real pretty on her."

"I'll just bet some of these are meant for your mother, aren't they?"

"Well, yes ma'am, but I already set aside a couple of pieces I hoped she would like." Solomon admitted sheepishly.

Mrs. Mary turned and looked over her glasses. "Young Solomon, I greatly admire a man who thinks softly of his women folk." He had to admit he liked Mrs. Mary's approval.

It was after noon before Mrs. Dudley and Solomon concluded their business, both satisfied with their goods and prices. "Mrs. Dudley," Solomon began timidly. "I don't mean to be what my Mama calls forward or nothin', but I wonder would you be pleased to take this from me?"

Mary Dudley had been a sturdy, hard working body all of her life. She loved a laugh but had seen plenty of suffering. The Dudley place was considered quite prosperous but she hadn't experienced luxuries. She wasn't often moved to speechlessness or teary eyes. In this remarkable young colored boy's outstretched hand was a decorative hair comb. It was medium in size and looked sturdy enough to corral even her thick, unruly hair. Silently, she reached to touch the smooth amber and gold ornament. "Tortoise shell?" she finally asked.

"Yes'm. Least that's what they sold it to me for. I don't know as I ever saw any so I couldn't be sure. Just knew I liked it and thought about the color of your hair when I saw it." He remembered himself and quickly added, "No disrespect, ma'am."

"None taken, my boy, none taken." Mrs. Dudley held the comb up to the sun which made the polished shell glow. She gently fingered the delicate floral design across its spine then looked right into his eyes. "Solomon, I don't have to tell you that we owned slaves. I like to think we were decent and fair, but it was owning them still." She struggled to find her words. "Never once have I seen even those I have been closest to through the eyes I see you with. This is a beautiful gift and I'll wear it for my best."

Reclaiming her typical tone, Mrs. Dudley laughed easily, her eyes blazing with spirit. "I hope to meet your mother, Solomon, for she is sure to be a fine woman." The look on the boy's face was agreement enough. He didn't need to say that Lela Freeman was the finest woman he would ever know. Mrs. Dudley insisted that he come to the back porch for some lunch. He knew he couldn't refuse so he ate as much as he could from the plate she handed him. The best part was the cool lemonade. *I wonder does Mama know how to make lemonade?* He struggled to get the food down, though, as he was tired and edgy all at the same time.

Solomon knew he should be relieved that things had gone as well as they had and that they were only a few days from home. He spent the afternoon helping Manuel rearrange the goods in the wagons and should have been dead tired. Maybe he was so jittery because he'd slept very little since they'd recrossed the prairie coming north. In the long, dark nights in front of him, all he saw was an image of Big Jim sinking into a gray-brown oozing mud. He just couldn't enter the shadows to face it. And it didn't seem like the brightly kerchiefed girl would move out of the shadows toward him.

The next morning the wagons were some lighter, thanks to Mrs. Dudley's purchases. Every creature, from men to horses, was pleased about that. With good-byes and see-you-next-years all around, the wagons headed northward. As they moved out, Solomon swung wide of the wagons on the side of the yard, scanning the area. Yes, there peeking from behind the wash house was a shy face. Swamp Foot didn't stop but did slow considerably at his rider's signal. They made eye contact as horse and boy approached. Then, too soon, the yellow kerchief disappeared into the shadows.

CHAPTER TWELVE

It took three days to travel north and west to Ft. White. The trip could have been made in two if they pushed, but it proved profitable to wind around and stop at farms along the way. The woods and crossroad villages were full of people hungry for new and unusual things even if they were only able to look and more than not they bought enough little bits to make most stops worthwhile. Sometimes deals were bartered with hand crafted or grown items that added variety to the wagons' merchandise. There was no plan to stop for more than a short overnight anyplace until they reached the Freeman place. But stop they did.

They were close enough to home to almost smell the cook fire and as they approached a place that was set back from the road a ways and Solomon, Slim, and Cookie agreed it probably wasn't even worth their time. "Don't look none too prosperous, Solomon," said Slim as he craned his neck to see the place a little better.

"It don't at that," agreed Cookie. "'Course you really can't tell much by the looks of it." They left the decision to Solomon who deemed it worth a stop to refresh themselves and water the animals at least. Then, if they sold something they sold something but it wouldn't be a wasted stop.

What they found, when they approached at a cautious speed, was a series of wagons and tents arranged like a military camp next to a nearly completed structure. It was a busy place with a white man and several coloreds from about Solomon's age to full grown men hammering, sawing, and hollering instructions to each other. Stopping well out from the camp, Solomon called out, "Hello the camp!"

"Wagons, comin', Boss!" called out one young laborer. Close enough now to see the homestead, Solomon noted that, by local standards, it was grand: two stories, large porches on both levels, and plenty of room to house the brood that scurried toward the wagons.

The man who must be Boss left his work and walked with an uneven gait toward the halted company. "Afternoon to you," the man said, wiping his sweaty face with a red bandana.

The fact that he knew as trail boss this was his job, and that he'd been boss for these months now, didn't make Solomon one bit more comfortable doing it. "Afternoon, sir," he said dismounting Swamp Foot and removing his hat.

The man's face showed his surprise at Solomon taking the lead with plenty of white men right there who could take the lead, but he nodded and waited without saying anything more.

"My name is Solomon Freeman, sir, and we're headed home after three months of cow hunting and selling. This outfit belongs to Mr. Pete Harker up to Madison."

"You are in Mr. Harker's employ?" the man asked.

Solomon nodded and motioned for those on horseback to step down.

Being a slight man, he looked up at Solomon. "My name is Thomas Getzen, late of Edgefield District, South Carolina." Waving his hand in a broad gesture he explained, "This doesn't look like much now, but give us a couple of years and you'll see that it will become a farm of great industry."

Trying to say something polite, the boy boss observed, "Nice place you picked, here with all these shade trees." Solomon found it difficult to read this Mr. Getzen. And what kind of name was that? Not that Solomon had heard all that many names in his whole life, but he'd certainly never heard that one before. "I wonder   could you spare some water for the men and animals before we move on?"

"No reason why not," Getzen replied after a pause. "No reason at all." He directed the men toward the well which must have been the first thing they constructed. It was getting so late in the season that Solomon wondered if they might be sorry they hadn't built shelter first. Looking toward the wagons curiously Getzen asked, "Did you have a successful trip?"

"Well, yessir, I'd like to say we did. Lots of goods here should you want to take a look." It was clear that Mr. Getzen did want to look and the men untied and turned back the canvas covering the goods in each wagon before they went to the well. They
would bring buckets of water back to the animals.

"Well, yessir, I'd like to say we did. Lots of goods here should you want to take a look." It was clear that Mr. Getzen did want to look and the men untied and turned back the canvas covering the goods in each wagon before they went to the well. They would bring buckets of water back to the animals.

Solomon knew he needed to do business any time the opportunity came so Manuel took Swamp Foot and Solomon walked with Getzen to inspect the goods. In just a short time, Manuel returned with cups of cool water for both Solomon and Mr. Getzen and a bucket full for Swamp Foot.

"I know it's hard to believe today, but this will soon be a bustling and thriving farm. The house isn't finished yet but I just couldn't wait longer to go back to South Carolina to bring my wife and three children to our new home. I don't think I should pass up the chance to buy things that would benefit our new household." As though they knew what Mr. Getzen would be saying, his wife and children arrived in a swarm. Solomon noted it was probably a good idea the house was so large as there obviously would be more than three children. And soon.

Solomon thought this Mr. Getzen was acting a little fancy and standoffish – prosperous maybe, but not at Pete's level. *Mama says don't judge and me and the crew aren't exactly to be expected either.*

It was a successful stop, though, because Mr. Getzen's surety that his farm would be a success led him to buy a few tools and farm implements. In fact, Solomon had to insist that a few items be held from sale or the little man would have taken them all.

His wife and daughters bought yard goods and household items. The girls each selected a fancy hair ribbon and Mr. Getzen presented a bracelet to his wife with surprising sentimentality. To reward himself and his men, the wagons were lightened by several bottles of rum and a few aromatic Cuban cigars.

"Now, Solomon," he said. "Is it likely that you'll pass this way again next fall gathering a herd?"

"Well, sir," Solomon answered truthfully. "That all depends on Mr. Pete Harker. He's the one owns this outfit. He just couldn't make this trip so he made me trail boss."

"Did he now? And isn't that a site," Getzen's cynicism whispered. "A mite young for such a job, aren't you?" Composing himself, the man asked seriously.

Chuckling at himself, Solomon admitted, "Yessir, that's pretty well how I felt 'bout it but ever'body agreed and I didn't have much choice." The boy continued. "We put together a drive every year these past several and I'd expect Mr. Pete to be along next year. I'll admit it ain't been quite the same without him and I'd be pleased to be shed of the boss hat."

"Well then, I'll expect you to see that Mr. Harker passes by here next year. There will be a herd for you to pick up."

"I'll let him know, sir, I surely will," Solomon promised. This Mr. Getzen was pretty sure of himself -- more sure than it looked like he should be with only a couple of old milk cows in sight. It was late enough in the day that they planned to move just a few miles further west and set camp at the clearest, purest river Solomon could imagine with a name he couldn't say. He called it Itchy for short. Solomon rode alongside the chuck wagon. "Mr. Cookie?"

"Yeah, boy," Cookie muttered, age and exhaustion showing after several months on the trail. "What's on your mind?" Cookie could always tell when Solomon was worried.

"How'd Mr. Getzen seem to you?" "Cock sure of himself, for sure, why?"

"I can see him with the house and all his family. But do you think he'll have a herd next year? Can he get somethin' goin' in a year? Less than a year even?"

Cookie scratched at his whiskery face. He was clean shaven all the rest of the year and by this time his trail beard was too long, bristly, and tiresome. "I don't know, boy, I just don't know. 'Pears he has some men and he's got a lot of saw timber. He's high spoken, alright. Must have schooling. Must have money, too." Looking at Solomon curiously, Cookie asked, "Why's this eatin' you so much?"

"Don't know, Mr. Cookie. Not really." Solomon had slowed Swamp Foot so much Cookie finally just pulled the wagon to a stop. Solomon faced his friend. "Just thinkin' on our first year, I reckon. Blind man could see Mr. Getzen has things we didn't. But to think he could have the whole house, barns, herd, crops . . . all in one year?"

"I know what you mean.You're seeing a fine example of how life and the world don't treat us fair."

Cookie reached into the canvas bag hanging just behind him and offered Solomon a strip of hard tack. "See, son, it don't matter how much we got, somebody's got more. And don't matter how little we got, somebody's got less. No, sir, 'taint fair, but seems that's the way of things."

"We worked so hard these years – 'most five years. Be five years come spring." Solomon's frustration muted him.

"Solomon, you got to stop comparing. You and your Mama and Papa started out with little of nothing best I can tell. A few seeds, a few tools, and a little provision. The three of you claimed your farm and built and worked it."

"Yes, sir, we did that. Still doin' that."

"And you' go right on doing that, too. I imagine Mr. Getzen and lots of others come down here lately got a whole lot more than the Freemans. But what y'all have done is to be proud of." Solomon didn't look convinced. "You got a floor and a roof. You got food to eat and clothes on your backs. You make enough crops to keep you from this year to next. You got a fine family and good prospects for keeping on with just what you done so far, just growin' a little at a time."

Cookie paused for a couple of sips from a canteen and passed it over to Solomon. "Boy, you gonna have your place free and clear and all yours in just a few months. You don't owe a soul, do you?" The boy shook his head. "It ain't so much how much you got as how you got it and far as I can see the Freemans got theirs just the right way."

"Thanks, Mr. Cookie. I reckon you must be right." Solomon spurred Swamp Foot and moved away from the chuck wagon. Cookie popped the reins to spur the mules and the wagon moved out to catch up with the others, sure that Solomon now had more to sort out now than when he'd asked his first question.

"It's alright, Solomon," Cookie whispered. "You just startin' to think 'bout things a man ain't found answers to in all man's years. You ponder all you want. Just don't let it take you over."

After leaving the Getzen place, the drive stopped only at houses visible from the road. So close to home they could smell Lela's biscuits, there was no following divergent roads even when they knew they led to houses. Solomon wasn't the only one moving a little faster as they approached the Freeman place. The whole crew was ready for a real meal and a day or two's rest. It would take more than that to fully recover from several hard, monotonous months on the trail.

Well on the outskirts of the farm, Harry and Shorty were the first faces they saw and they made no secret that they were both glad to see the drovers return and even more glad to be on their way out of there. Neither would sign on with Pete Harker again -- at least not for this. They might work for him in Madison where they'd work for him not a bunch of darkies.

The two men, always choosing work away from the homestead when possible, fell in behind the wagons, mules pulling tall straight oak trees about a foot in diameter. As far as Harry and Shorty were concerned, those trees could stay in the yard until they rotted; they knew they weren't turning them into firewood.

The rattle of several wagons was a good warning that someone was approaching the house and Lela stood on the edge of the porch drying her hands by the time they rolled into the yard. She screamed so loudly that Sarah awoke from her nap and screeched even louder. Lela dashed inside, whisked the baby up, and dashed back into the yard. There was great uproar all around as men leapt off wagons and horses feeling as though they had returned home somehow. Shortly after Solomon let his mother's feet return to the ground after a big bear hug, his father came racing into the yard on Sally, fear written all over his face.

"Lord have mercy, boy," Moses said huffing and puffing. "I thought somebody had yore Mama and sister for sure."

Gripping his father's outstretched arms, Solomon laughed. "Somebody does have Mama and Sarah, Papa." He reached to his right and enveloped them protectively. "Just never know how you miss a place, do you, Papa?"

"Never do, son," Moses said with a face splitting grin. It was good to have his family whole again. The hubbub increased as the Freemans turned to welcome the rest of the men and for the next hour there was a quick passing of the water dipper and uncovering the wagons for inspection.

Solomon was pleased with the selling they had done on the way home, but knew he had plenty of merchandise for Cookie and Slim to take two stock wagons and the chuck wagon packed high and tight on to Madison for Pete to disburse and still have enough for both Mr. Hart and the tiny store in Fayettetown. After the big sale at the Getzen place, the wagons had been repacked so Solomon knew what was to stay with his family was in one wagon and the sale and trade goods in the others.

Lela immediately moved toward the wagon destined for town and the men untied its canvas cover. Solomon moved to explain to his mother than her things were in the other wagon but Moses' grasp stopped him. "She know which wagon which, boy," the man explained. "But you know yore Mama and good as you be, you can't be trusted to pick everything just right for a woman."

Sarah mimicked their laughter as Solomon agreed, "I should have known Mama would have to see for herself that there's nothing in that wagon she can't do without." Solomon moved to join his mother so he could guide her through the wagons. Nothing much was unloaded. This was just the time to look. The boy knew that by mid morning the next day, Lela would have gone through both wagons carefully and made her choices. Just like all the rest, that merchandise would be duly paid for out of Solomon's wages and recorded in his little notebook. He knew he would still have some cash to help the family get through the year safely.

Hours later, in the chilled dark of winter, the company enjoyed a venison stew they were sure tasted better than New Orleans' very best restaurant could offer. Not that any of them had been to New Orleans but they'd heard tell. Questions and answers and stories told from all perspectives swirled around the larger-than-usual cook fire. Only Harry and Shorty declined the jolly gathering, choosing to sit on the far end of the porch eating in lantern light. "Their loss," Slim observed under his breath as he bobbed his head in their direction.

"Yeah," Cookie agreed. "I thought those two hyenas would change their minds after being around the Freemans all this time."

Manuel, who sat on Cookie's other side whispered, "I do not see how any man could have a hard heart for the Freemans." He shook his head and crossed himself quickly. "El Diablo is in them, no?"

By the time clean up after a late supper was done everyone just wanted to bed down. There would be time tomorrow for Lela to make serious selections at the rolling store. The men would enjoy stretching their legs and using unaccustomed muscles chopping word and making an addition on the bunk house.

Her routine chores didn't suffer the next morning, because Cookie was up even earlier than Lela so she didn't have to cook breakfast. "What a luxury, Cookie! I feel like royalty!" she exclaimed as she sipped a cup of strong trail coffee.

"As you should, Lela." Cookie and Pete were the only ones who called Lela so familiarly. "I know you won't get to your shopping," Cookie chuckled, "until your work is caught up so you just move along. I want to see what you find to like in those wagons."

First Lela attacked the wagon Solomon had set aside for his family, anxious to see just how her boy perceived their needs. He knew them, alright. And Moses would be mightily moved when he saw what Solomon brought him. Charlie helped her unload bundles, barrels, and boxes so she could decide what to keep and where to keep it.

"Have mercy, Charlie," she said breathlessly, "it could take days to put these things to rights."

Charlie, having lost no humor when he lost his hand, guffawed. "You're right about that Miss Lela. That boy spent near all his time findin' things for you and Moses. Oh, and young Sarah there." Like a carnival magician, Charlie rummaged in a hard sided valise and, with a flourish, pulled out a doll. Not corn husks or stuffed remnants but a real store bought doll which he gently offered to Sarah. Momentarily,
Charlie worried that she didn't squeal – her universal sign of excitement. She slowly reached out to touch the doll's smooth face and long hair. Hesitantly, Sarah took the doll in her arms held her in a gentle embrace and let out the biggest squeal her little lungs would produce. Charlie shouted over the girl, "Good healthy lungs she got, ain't it?"

Next Charlie opened a wooden crate in which she found treasures of fabrics, thread, buttons, and other sewing and mending supplies. "No ma'am, 'sides shoppin' I don't think he advantaged what the island had to offer atall." Having a second thought he quickly added, "And that speaks right well of what you and Moses been teaching the boy, it does. Us men didn't much need to partake of the island such like we did." The more he said the deeper he dug. The deeper he dug the faster he worked.

Embarrassed right along with Charlie Lela changed the subject. "Why so much, Charlie? Some of this should go to Mr. Hart's store."

"You'd have to consider that with Solomon, Miss Lela, but he put a lot of store in finding everything you needed or wanted. Might you could go easy on passing any of these goods along."

He was right, of course, and Lela put a gentle hand on Charlie's stump. "Thank you, Charlie. We've scratched out so long that my practical side comes out too strongly sometimes and of course you're right. Every one of these items will find good use I'm sure." Laughing, she added, "It might take years to use them all, but they'll see good use!"

Hating to store things away without Moses seeing them, Lela arranged her supplies along a wall in their house. His things she left in the wagon were for him to discover, especially the large canvas covered object at the very back of the wagon.

Angus and Slim worked hard until early afternoon when they asked Lela what she had in mind for supper. She was just about to put a large smoked ham on a spit over the fire.

"Oh, Miz Lela, that's too much on you. Let us bring you some fish."

She looked suspicious. "Are you two telling me that you can catch enough fish to keep this crew from going hungry?" She laughed and advised, "You'd better take two poles apiece so you can fish two-handed." After her jest, she added her thanks for their intentions. "We'll just see if we have crispy fish tonight or some cornmeal mush because on your guarantee I don't plan to cook anything else!"

Lela was nearly finished showing Moses the yard goods, kitchen tools, and canned and dry food stuffs as Solomon stood aside beaming. She admired and stroked the soft, sweet blanket and ruffled dress that she knew Sarah would love instantly. She was born in the wrong time and place for it but Lela was sure that she had a little girl who was very fond of all types of frippery. "Ain't seen such pure pleasure on a face in a coon's age, boy," said Charlie elbowing Solomon in the ribs. "Yessir, some satisfaction seein' them you love in such pleasure, ain't it?" Solomon could only nod, fearful that his voice would give away his near to overflowing emotions.

As Lela moved to put some of the gifts away, Moses approached his son. "That's a fine thing you've done, Solomon. Your Mama been without finery – shoot, ain't even finery she missed but pure d necessaries – too long." In the most affectionate gesture his father had ever displayed toward his son, Moses tenderly wrapped his improved but still weakened arm around Solomon's shoulders and repeated. "A fine thing, Son." The lump in the boy's throat just got bigger. They moved at once to help Lela stash away her goods to move from the unaccustomed closeness.

"Papa," Solomon explained quickly, "you know there's stuff in the wagon for you, too. I couldn't forget you. It's just that Mama . . ." Solomon didn't quite know how to continue.

"I know that, boy," his father assured him. "And you done 'xact right thing treatin' your Mama first." Moses rubbed his hands together with anticipation. "Now her things out, I plan to spend the better part of tomorrow mornin' emptyin' that wagon out. Don't you worry I won't see my part 'out you there so I'll wait 'til you finished your breakfast, and I know it be just as good as your Mama's."

Sure enough the men returned straining under the weight of the line of fish they caught. Lela rushed them to get the fish cleaned so they could eat supper before full moonrise. Murphy and George gravitated to like minds and ate apart from the fire with Harry and Shorty. As soon as they stacked their plates near

the wash tub they removed themselves to their bedrolls, mimicking and sneering at the congenial company surrounding the fire.

"Mrs. Freeman, 'tis a verra long time indeed since I hae a meal of such quality," Angus announced formally. "Though I wondered might we reach starvation ere we ate 'tis that late." The Scotsman took a long pull on the pipe he smoked only rarely and looked at the clear winter sky. "Perhaps not a habit, no, but there is something fay calm and comforting enjoying a fine meal in the fire's glow."

"Thank you, Mr. Angus," Lela answered as she and Cookie continued clearing and washing their tin plates. "And aren't you the poet this evening!"

"Ah 'tis the curse of this infernal Scottish blood in me veins and the Highland heather in me heart I suppose. Betimes there's nae stopping it."

Adding just the right end to the night, Manuel picked his guitar in gentle rhythm. Several other voices joined his soft hum and provided background when he began to sing the poignant words. At least now Solomon knew enough Spanish to know they were poignant. The rest felt the magic of the music. When the last note was sounded the company silently moved to their separate places and slept soundly having enjoyed the world's best sedative – tranquil pleasant company.

For all of his silent strength, those at the breakfast fire knew Moses wasn't gobbling a biscuit and slurping the blistering coffee because he was so hungry. The drovers who had remained at the Freeman's wanted to watch Moses almost as much as Lela and Solomon did.

In accord, they left the fire, thanking Lela for breakfast, and saw to the early morning feeding and egg gathering. Solomon even helped Lela clean the dishes and in a trice they were pushing Moses toward the mysterious wagon.

"Lawdy," he said, hiding his own excitement unsuccessfully. "You think it was Christmas at the big house, all this do-dah goin' on." When he reached the wagon, the company circled, waiting. Once he began it was hard to slow Moses down and Lela had never seen such grinning and exclaiming. Overalls, boots, long johns, and even a suit of dress clothes were uncovered first. "When in God's big green world am I gon' wear duds like this?"

"Cut a fine figure, Papa. Mama has another surprise for later and you two can get all dressed up and dance in the firelight one night soon." Supported by an encouraging chorus, Solomon urged, "Get on with it, Papa, there's more." Next, out came hand tools, tack, and a brand new rifle and cartridges.

Moses held the gun up tentatively letting the metal of the barrel shine in the early morning sun. The watchers held their breath knowing that the old shotgun that exploded in his face was never far from Moses' memory when he had to fire a weapon. He knew it was a fine gun and a helpful tool so he tried to greet it cheerfully. "Fine gun this is. Be a big help with huntin', ceptin' I best be shootin' sharp 'cause this don't allow no excuses for missin' nothing'."

Cookie stepped forward to relieve the man of the rifle and Moses shrugged and shook his head in disbelief. "Son, ain't no man ever had a better family nor a son to give such bounty. Can't think nobody has had a bigger or better surprise than this."

Moses couldn't imagine anything more but Solomon pushed him to throw back the canvas just behind the seat of the wagon. The big man gasped emotionally – proud, excited, humiliated. It was a two-furrow, seated plow that Sudie and Sally could pull. Exactly the same item he had ordered from Dukes. Tears welling up, weeks before he had accepted that the one he ordered would never arrive. He looked at Lela and saw that she felt exactly as he did. She moved to his side and whispered an intense message, "Be pleased, Moses, no need to do anything else."

His lame arm encircled his wife and he murmured back, "Can't do it, Lela. I got to tell him. It was a terrible foolish thing and just ain't a secret I can keep."

"A secret **we** can't keep, husband," she assured him. The festive mood had evaporated and only Moses and Lela knew why.

"Come to the fire, boy, we got to tell you." He hushed his son's confused questions and they moved toward the fire, the drovers tactfully moving toward the stock pens. "Nope," Moses called to them, "you few 'bout as much family as we got – along with Pete. No reason you shouldn't hear what we got to tell."

Assuring Solomon that what he was about to hear in no way diminished the sheer pleasure and pride he felt for his son's thoughtful generosity, the story came out slowly. Together Moses and Lela told the story of their encounter with the "gentleman," Mr. Josiah Dukes. "Don't know which I hate most – that I fell for that fancy big talk of his or that in these times we can't even trust our own kind."

Disgust hurled in all directions across the fire. "Damn carpetbaggers," Slim spat. "Bad 'nough being caught in war nobody could come out winning. Ain't not one of us here safe from that war and these times and most of us woulda fell for just the same kind of double-cross." He spoke for them all.

The rest of the day was spent putting the new goods in order and tending to usual chores, but without the usual comfort and good spirits felt on the Freeman place. It was the last day the extra hands would be on the place and at least most of the crew hoped to do those last few things that would set their friends well for fast approaching winter. Lela sped through the day aimed at preparing a special farewell dinner and Cookie was by her side to do it. They all felt the residue of the morning's revelation and facing the clear knowledge that each man is a fool in his own way. Such admission required privacy of thought.

Just past dawn the next morning the drovers pulled out – the new men pulled their pay and scattered their own ways, with none to regret they were probably not to be seen again. The old crew took two half loaded wagons to finish peddling goods into Madison to give Pete his part of the payout. They traveled nervously with so much value at stake. At the same time, Solomon left in the Freemans' wagon headed for New Troy and Fayettetown. These were the goods he paid for personally and he was anxious to see if he had chosen well. If none of the merchants wanted his goods he would know that he would need to quit business and stick to cow hunting.

Just before leaving, Cookie asked Lela about the subtle change in Solomon. "Yes, Cookie, I noticed. It's of a sudden, though, and I just don't know what to make of it."

Cookie explained that he had noticed moments of despondence in the boy on the trail but accounted for it by the inordinate responsibility and pressure that had been placed on the boy. "Maybe Pete – maybe all of us – misjudged Solomon. Oh, not that he couldn't handle the drive but that it wouldn't be good for him."

CHAPTER THIRTEEN

January, 1871 -- Christmas passed and the fresh, frigid new year had just begun. Pete, Cookie, and Slim arrived in the mid-afternoon. It was an unusual time of year for the Freeman's to see Pete, but he'd not been there since before the cattle drive and he was always welcome. It was a quick visit that would change the Freeman farm permanently.

Supper was eaten and cleaned up, and the friends had just about caught up on their news. Pete stood and stretched then asked Solomon to stand, too. Something was cagey about the way Pete surveyed the boy, apparently checking his growth and alertness from when he'd seen him last. Moses and Lela were so focused on Pete and Solomon that they didn't notice that Slim had slipped away from the fire and their other friends were on edge.

"Solomon, you've certainly gotten taller and you handled that last drive well," Pete began. "Do you think you've grown up as a man, too?"

"Well, Pete," Solomon hadn't used a title with Pete for nearly a year now, "I wouldn't say I'm a man quite, but I'm workin' real hard to do my part."

"I know you are, son, and I want to give you something that will require every bit as much care, practice, and responsibility as that whip you've mastered." Looking deeply into the boy's eyes Pete nodded his head almost imperceptibly and reached his hand behind his back. When the hand came back into sight, it held a wriggling, squiggling, growling ball of fur. Solomon looked at the little beast that was controlled only with both of Pete's large hands, then he looked, wide-eyed, into his friend's face. "He's yours, Solomon, all yours."

Scooping up the puppy, Solomon could only sputter. "Oh, Pete, mine? All mine?" He held the little multi-colored whirlwind up close and it licked his face. The whole company laughed and Moses and Lela couldn't possibly have forbidden this gift if they had wanted to.

"What'll you name him, Solomon?" Lela asked, reaching to caress the soft fur. She took the pup's face in her hands and looked him eye to eye. "Did you know you're so ugly you're cute!"

"I don't know, Mama," Solomon answered. "Maybe in a couple of days he'll do something that'll make his name clear."

"Lots of extra responsibility, son, raisin' a dog." Moses' warning wasn't unkind, but it was firm. "And pup can do harm, lots of harm. You see you get control right off so he don't do no destruction."

"Yessir, Papa, I'll look after him real close," the boy promised.

It seemed that the puppy couldn't last a minute without a growl, snarl, or yammer of some kind. "You think you can roar, Tiger?" Solomon asked. Out came a howl bigger than his body should have produced and it was settled. Instantly, Tiger was a grand source of entertainment, endearment, and exasperation. He was smart and, for a pup, displayed a fair ability to ignore distractions and focus on Solomon's commands. Any time Solomon was up and about, Tiger was by his side learning his voice, hand signals, and basic commands. For such an active dog he was surprisingly gentle with Lela and Sarah who adored him, although the little girl was a bit leary of most other animals. Wisely, he decided early on to avoid Moses when possible, sensing that this great big human didn't have much patience with learning pups.

The problems came when he wasn't with Solomon. There were hundreds of curiosities and Tiger felt obliged to learn about them all. His favorite sports were nipping at the heels of Sunny, Sudie, and Swamp Foot and chasing chickens and piglets. Instinct told him to avoid the temperamental sows, playing with the pigs only when the sows weren't in evidence. Tiger's efforts to protect the place were appreciated though misguided. As he stormed through Lela's garden for the third night, he reached the limit.

Tiger bounded happily toward Solomon as soon as the boy left the porch on his way to the privy and the boy knew he and Tiger were in for it. On his way back to the house they were met by his mother. "Solomon, either you get that dog under control or he's gone, do you hear?"

"Yes ma'am, Mama, I'll take care of it."

"You'd better find a way to take care of it. I don't care if he thinks he's doing a good thing chasing foxes or whatever he thought he saw, we can't do without this garden." She turned on her heel and went back into the house where Solomon heard pans framming and bamming. Never a good sign.

Solomon immediately turned and knelt in front of the dog who was considerably larger than when he arrived. Tiger's head drooped. Solomon figured the dog didn't know quite what he had done wrong but was pretty sure Tiger knew that he had done wrong aplenty. Grabbing each side of the scruff of Tiger's neck, Solomon looked the dog hard in the eyes and growled low but clear reprimand. "Bad. Bad dog." Tiger wrinkled his brow and stared right back into his master's eyes. "You get in Mama's garden just one more time and you have to leave here and I don't think neither one of us can bear that."

Solomon stood, bent to hold the dog's collar and took him around the perimeter of the garden all the while saying firmly, "No. No garden. No. Stay out. No." He sat the dog just at the edge of the crumpled little fence and told him to stay. Solomon righted as much of the garden as could be righted, sure to position himself so that he could see Tiger. A couple of times Tiger stood and took a step forward and heard a sharp, "No! Stay!"

By the end of that very day, Solomon had taken Tiger to New Troy with him, tying the dog to the wagon while he ran his errands, and began refortifying the garden. The next day Tiger stayed on the outside of the fence, following Solomon and watching him add more posts, dig a trench a few inches deep all along the fence line, and put up sturdy chicken wire. The last step was to refill the trench and firmly stomp it down. Perhaps the hardest part was putting in a gate on each end of the garden that was as protective as the fence line but easy for his mother to use. "There, boy," Solomon pronounced. "If critters get in this fence, they 'bout near deserve a bite or two." He knew it had to protect the garden from both wild marauders and his beloved Tiger.

Within a few months even Lela grudgingly admitted that the dog had improved and learned more than she'd thought he could. He practiced herding the pigs and chickens instead of chasing them, a great help every afternoon when both were called to their protective pens for the night. After many training sessions, on command, he could catch a chicken or rabbit and hold it until someone took it from him. He soon learned that he would be well rewarded when he behaved and when he helped provide food for "his people."

Tiger's hardest lesson was respecting the whip without fearing it. When Solomon first demonstrated it Tiger was not quite afraid, but wary. Over time he learned to follow "his boy's" hand and vocal signals. The little notch in his left ear taught him where to stand to avoid being clipped by the whip. It would take much more time before Tiger was ready for a drive.

CHAPTER FOURTEEN

Early Spring 1871 -- The Freemans sat under the stars and Moses lit one of his precious Cuban cigars, bounty from Solomon doing business with Cuban ship captains. He had noted the routine of the farm closing in on Solomon and offered a solution. "Son, you lookin' a mite itchy."

Startled, Solomon squirmed a little not realizing his feelings were so obvious. "Well, yes sir, I reckon maybe so, Papa." He wasn't sure whether Moses was mad or might be learning his son's changeable nature. "Maybe it's just a little cabin fever after the winter." Solomon hoped that was adequate explanation because he wasn't even able to explain his feelings most of the time.

After a long, thoughtful draw on the fragrant cigar Moses nodded. "I don't wonder. Might be we could use some fresh meat and this be a good time for it. 'Nother few weeks spring plantin' be on us and be no time for it." Solomon held his breath. "I'd say you want to take a ramble a few days, this be time for it."

Lela's eyes were locked onto her son's face and the surprise and relief on it made her smile, thankful that Moses had taken such a bold step. It was hard for Moses to understand Solomon's differences. "I know you're self sufficient, son, but I'll bake up extra biscuits in the morning for a little travel sack."

"Thank you, Mama," Solomon murmured. "And I'll bring back somethin' real good, Papa." He could say no more.

After hardly sleeping at all Solomon gulped a couple of biscuits and ham for breakfast, made quick good-byes, and mounted Swamp Foot to begin his adventure. "I'll be back in a few days, Mama, don't you worry."

Tiger seemed to know that something was happening and that it must be exciting. He ran from one to the other of the family, prancing and licking hands. Moses even reached down to give him a rough pat on the head and spoke to the dog in a whisper. "You big 'nough to earn your keep now, dog. You see to that boy, you hear?" It was the first time Moses had ever paid him any attention and Tiger looked at the big man calmly and seriously as though he knew this would be a test for him.

For the first time in a long time Solomon began to relax. By the end of the first day he sat comfortably in the saddle as he, Swampie, and Tiger rambled along the river southward then west a bit. He stopped to fish, cook on a spit over the open fire, and rest whenever the notion struck him. Drowsily rubbing Tiger's ears in the afternoon sun he said, "Ain't this just what we been needin', boy? Ain't you been ructious, too?" Tiger yawned in response, curled up next to Solomon and joined his boy in slumber.

Before long, Tiger's eyes opened and his ears pricked. An observer wouldn't have noticed that the dog had moved a muscle. He couldn't place the sense he had or from which direction it came, but he knew he was supposed to be ready.

Before dog or boy could know it, three men jumped them pinning Solomon hard to the ground. Tiger sprang up and latched onto the fat calf of an even fatter man's leg. Leaving Solomon to his friends, the attacker tried to shake the dog off. Seeing that wouldn't work, and dancing in pain, he balled up his chubby fist and slugged the dog right between the eyes. A brief whimper was Tiger's only response

In the seconds before Solomon was fully alert he had been completely subdued, trussed up like a hog, and thrown on his stomach. He couldn't think why Swampie hadn't sounded an alarm – he was usually watchful.

Solomon couldn't see that the horse had been led away and tied in the woods so he couldn't interfere.

Out of the corner of one eye Solomon saw an unmoving Tiger and thrashed to reach him. It was immediately evident that the more he struggled against the ropes, the tighter they got. He would have to think clearly and work smart if he was to get out of this fix. He thought his heart would burst not being able to tell whether Tiger was injured or dead.

In that agonizing moment Solomon knew who he was dealing with. It was Pork and his friends. Nasty, smelly, repulsive – they had almost raped his mother not long after the Freemans had established their homestead. Bile rose in the boy's throat at the thought of that day. Rough hands sat him up, stood back, and laughed. Pork sneered, baring his rotting teeth. "Lookie here, lookie here, boys. He's growed a mite but it's our boy alright." He strutted around Solomon who knelt as still and quietly as he could, knowing he must be patient and wait for his opportunity. "I do believe we got us a little money-makin' proposition here and no big man with a whip nowhere."

The entire company hooted. "How you 'spect to do that, Pork?" asked one of the less enterprising of the group.

"Well, I tell ya," Pork began, spitting brown juice not on but just in front of Solomon. "I heard a man over to the old Jenkins place was acceptin' laborers and we might just have one fer 'im." Pork's emphasis on the word laborers was ominous.

Still trussed and thrown belly down on Swampie's back, Solomon bumped and swung head down for what seemed like hours. He had no idea what direction they were going. His head pounded and he eventually vomited everything he had eaten the last two days, the sour bile sticking in his throat and coating his mouth. His physical pain couldn't match his dread about Tiger's fate.

He was taken to what was now the Groaton place where Pork sold him for $120. The disoriented boy watched them ride out in glee as he was untied but firmly restrained and taken into a barn. True to his nature, though perhaps not the best approach to the situation, Solomon fought and struggled. He learned that got nothing but beatings and bruises.

Obviously strong, he was put to work in field and not allowed near Swampie. He lay awake at night wondering about his parents, his little sister, Tiger, and how in the world he would get his hands on his tack where he hoped his whip was still tied.

Despite his father's stories of past practices, the desperate boy tried escaping once. After all, he thought, slavery was over. Apparently somebody didn't note emancipation and, having left the north and taken over a small out-of-the way plantation in Taylor County, had his own plans for building a labor force.

Dragged back to the barn, Solomon felt cold, steely hatred brewing and vowed that he would get away and tend to Pork once and for all. He dreaded night when images of an inert cur dog filled his dreams.

After two weeks, Moses and Lela were frantic. They knew Solomon would never stay away so long on a ramble. This was well worth a rare visit to town where Moses inquired of Mr. Hart who had heard of a few unscrupulous land owners who didn't want to accept the war's end and used any means possible to get farm work done. Mr. Hart was kind enough to help Moses write to the only person they could think of who might be able to help. They could not accept that Solomon was lost to them.

Three weeks later, at the end of summer, Pete rode Diamond up to the bunk house showing signs of a long hard ride.

Lela dished up the last of the supper's stew and poured their friend a cup of coffee. Moses, Lela, and Sarah, who didn't understand what was going on but knew she missed her big brother, stared expectantly as Pete took a long sip of hot coffee.

"I'm sorry it took so long for me to get here." Looking at Moses he explained. "Your letter was waiting when I returned home from Savannah. I set out the next morning and spent a few days asking some discreet questions."

Impatient with worry Lela interrupted. "Did you get answers, Pete? Do you know where our boy is?"

Pete swallowed a big bite of stew and continued his explanation. "What I learned was that there are a few, thankfully very few, men who either to save their farms or plantations from ruin or who came from the north and took property over by basically kidnapping likely laborers."

"Here we thinkin' slavery over and find such as this goin' on." Moses could hardly contain his disdain. "Ain't right, Pete. Jus' ain't right."

"You're right Moses. This might as well be enslavement and it isn't right at all. That's at least part of what the fight was about. Seeing this kind of thing just makes all that death and loss worthless." Setting his empty plate down and rubbing his tired eyes, Pete observed, "But there will always be men who find some way to use others for their profit, no matter the right or wrong of it."

With a shudder of memory Lela voiced her prayer. "Lord, protect us from ever being so selfish or cruel."

Getting back to business, Moses asked, "But what can we do, Pete? Did you find out what we can do?"

"I'm not sure **we** need to do anything, Moses. I'm sorry to say that dealing with this kind of person won't go well if you're along." Moses' nod indicated that he knew exactly his friend was saying. Pete closed his eyes and clinched his teeth, sorry scenes replaying in his mind. "Shanghaied to a ship or a plow, it's all the same.

"You know what it be like, Pete . . .," whispered Moses. "We know you love that boy near 'bout much as me and his mama." Pete looked at Moses with glistening eyes and nodded. "We know you do right by him and we know our place be to stay here and pray."

Piecing together bits of information from Mr. Hart, others in New Town, and a few larger land owners beyond, Pete identified three possibilities. Though there were no eyewitness accounts, all were rumored to use various unscrupulous methods to operate farming operations profitably. With no way to rank them Pete decided to visit each place under the guise of bank investments, and it rankled him because he would never do business with people who dealt in abuse. Mr. Hart was the operator of the newly installed telegraph line so Pete sent word to Madison that Slim and Manuel should join him on the north edge of the one nearest New Town. He also planned for Angus and Charlie to come to the farm to help Moses catch up with spring planting. Solomon had been gone for almost two months already and there was no way to know how much longer it would be. The farm couldn't operate on its own. They knew without Pete's warning that Moses would insist they shouldn't have come, but they knew he needed the help.

The first plantation Pete, Slim, and Manuel reached was hardly large enough to be considered a plantation but the owner insisted on calling it that. He "employed" people he said were slaves who chose to stay with the land and continue working it on shares. The empty and hopeless faces he saw made him doubt that they enjoyed any freedom at all. With little suspicion Slim and Manuel moved around the place and among the people well enough to be sure that this wasn't the place they sought.

The party of three approached the second place, a larger more organized and apparently more prosperous plantation, noting the number of laborers there were. It would take a very large operation or an extremely wealthy man to support such a large labor force. He saw no chains, no individuals tied or restrained. He also saw very few women. This unnamed farm was distant from most rebuilding plantations of the region, an important level of security for the owner.

Pete was approaching the house when something caught his eye. On a small rise, the silhouette of a lone figure chopping wood. An elderly black man who wouldn't look at Pete's face reached to take Diamond's reins while a sullen white man approached, probably to find out the purpose of Pete's visit. He had no time to study the figure and it had been well over a month since the kidnapping, but Pete was almost certain it was Solomon.

Now Pete faced the hard part. Slim and Manuel, in the guise of body guards, studied every detail of the area within sight of the house as they ambled on different paths around the house and between barns. "Just stretchin' my legs," Slim explained to the unfriendly man who greeted them. "Been a long ride and Mr. Harker don't need us when he's safe inside talkin' business with your boss."

The challenger didn't like it, but Slim managed to continue his investigation aware that the man would never be far away. Manuel had an advantage because, like the Negroes, he could move almost invisibly with the assumption that they were simple-minded and harmless. Sometimes it was more helpful if he just played the part.

Approaching the horse paddock, Slim spied an animal that didn't seem to belong with the draft and high bred horses. Taking the offensive, he turned to his shadow, offered his hand and introduced himself. Surprised, the man did the same.

Leaning on the rail, Slim scanned the animals. "Good stock, Mr. Hughes, better than most around here." Hughes grunted. "Yessiree, Mr. Harker could do with a couple of those draft animals. Any for sale?"

"Price be put on most anything," Hughes muttered, offering no further conversation.

"And that little marshtackie there, ain't he a beaut. Broke is he?"

"Reckon so. Ain't bothered to try him," was the surly reply. Slim ambled around the paddock casually whistling an old Spanish tune then told Hughes he was headed back toward the pump to refresh before Harker had them on the road again. "That man don't know no quittin', he don't. Have to take ease whenever we can." Fed up with playing nursemaid to some simpleton body guard, Hughes mounted his horse and road toward the fields. Slim and Manuel had seen the person on the hill almost as soon as Pete had, but the figure was gone.

Guided by the whistled signal, Manuel met Slim at the pump and they spoke quietly as they drank and doused their heads. "I see many workers go into the big barn. An hombre with a shotgun walked with them and they don't come out," reported Manuel.

"Good eyes, amigo," Slim whispered as he stood to gaze toward the barn. There was little activity near the oversized barn so they moved in its direction. Peeking through broken slats at the rear of the barn the men could see that the workers indeed had gone in and wouldn't be coming out because they had been shackled to long chains and several attached to each support pole. They could walk some and reach water but that was about all. They found the face they sought -- the only person chained to the center post.

Hand signals set the plan and the two men slipped into dark corners of the building. Slim deftly overpowered the guard and tied him up, stuffing hay in his mouth so he couldn't sound an alarm when he came to. He and Manuel used the guard's keys to free every one of the astonished men. It was all the three friends could do not to break down when Solomon was unchained. The others just stood staring at Solomon as though waiting for direction. Solomon told them to stay silent and in the barn until he and his friends returned.

Pete, worrying about why Slim and Manuel were taking so long inspecting the place, had to work hard to convince Mathias Groaton that he was enjoying introductions and discussions of farming, banking, and anything else Pete could think of to kill time over whiskey. Pete decided that Groaton must have been given a big name to make up for his size. A scrawny, pale man with spear-like features, there was little attractive and a great deal repulsive to see in Mathias Groaton.

When Slim and Solomon finally entered the drawing room, Pete stood and caught his breath at the sight of the battered and bruised boy, knowing he couldn't have withstood much more abuse. While Manuel saddled Swampie and opened the barn doors so the laborers could leave, Slim stood watch at the doorway and Groaton stood dumbstruck.

This insolent darkie boy had walked right into his house, nodded at Harker, and sat right down on the divan like he belonged there. Pete knew Groaton was the kind of man who had others "handle" things so he didn't have to dirty his hands with the violence he pretended not to sanction.

Stretching to his fullest height, Pete faced Groaton and threatened the slick little man with the kind of slow, agonizing treatment he obviously directed his overseer to dispense. Pete's parting words were calm and subdued. "Groaton, if I ever – I mean ever – hear of you harming this young man or anyone remotely connected to him, you'll wish you had never seen this sorry excuse for a plantation." Groaton just blinked. "Furthermore, every hand on this place is now free – **again** – to return to their homes and families and your little scam will be reported to the authorities as soon as I can send a wire to Tallahassee." Pete's soft, controlled voice concluded, "Groaton, you have no idea how many eyes I have in this region. You misstep and I'll know. Trust me."

It was a full ten minutes after Pete and company left before Groaton regained himself enough to move. That was when he realized he was standing in a puddle.

The return home was purposefully slow to allow Solomon time for some of the cuts and bruises on his head and shoulders to at least fade a little. As his story unfolded his friends learned that he had been beaten with his own whip. In the course of tending his wounds, which were on the brink of infection, the men saw the extent of Solomon's treatment at the overseer's hand. Pete knew now that Solomon had experienced some of what both he and Moses had suffered at the hands of evil men. Moses was whipped as a young slave and Pete felt the cat-'o-nine-tails while he was pressed into service on a ship.

Pete pulled the whip from his gear and handed it over to Solomon. He hadn't known whether Solomon would want it back or not and it pleased him to know the experience didn't ruin his affinity for the weapon.

Solomon rode ahead in brooding silence. The only gleam to be seen in Solomon was his reunion with Swamp Foot.

Once they made camp Pete had a chance to talk to Slim. "Do you see it, Slim?"

"I do, Pete. I wish I didn't, but I do."

"A black vengeance flashes in Solomon's eyes in a way I'd not thought to see," Pete offered.

"Same as I see. This thing changed our boy, Pete, changed him for good," Slim observed sadly. "Ain't no man be beat and shackled and go unchanged."

Lela and Moses were nearly overcome when they saw Solomon riding into the yard. They had aged, he thought, and the place didn't look so great either. There was a tearful greeting and a quick, largely sanitized, recounting of Solomon's weeks away from them. Solomon, thinking that little Sarah was nudging his leg, reached down to pick her up. He fell on his knees just as thrilled to see Tiger as he had been to see his family.

"You alive, boy! How'd you find the way home?" Rubbing his furry friend's head Solomon noticed that Tiger wasn't as feisty as he remembered. Looking up at his mother with tears in his eyes he asked, "Mama, how long's Tiger been home? Was he hurt?"

"He staggered in here about three weeks ago, son." Lela knelt to massage the dog's back. "Looked like he'd gotten a pretty bad beating – an eye swollen shut and limping."

Moses joined his wife's explanation. "We figured broke ribs. Worse part was he was just so skinny and weak- like."

Solomon turned his gaze back to the dog and spoke. "You remember me, don't you, boy?"

"Oh, he remembers, alright, else he not be home," Moses assured Solomon. "'Pears he got a pretty good whack on the head, though, and he goes 'round sort of dizzy-headed sometime."

"Tiger, you tried to save me. You did good to find your way home. You just got to be well," Solomon commanded. The dog just nuzzled his boy's neck and lay down quietly. Solomon looked to his mother for reassurance. "I don't know, son. I just don't know," Lela said, continuing to rub Tiger gently. "He's a sight better than when he got here. Lord, I don't know how he made it. Eyes all swollen and scabbed up and poor old ribs just   showing
through."

"We just keep feedin' him and let him take his healin' how he needs to, son," Moses suggested. "Jus' got to hope he come back 'round."

Pete, Slim, and Manuel stayed on a couple of days and joined Charlie and Angus in the catching up they had been doing. "I thank you men," Pete told them sincerely, "I don't know how they'd make it through the season without your help and things are still a little behind." In addition to completing spring planting and mending things around the house and farm, they finished enlarging the smoke house and built a new privy. The men exchanged glances with Moses and Lela indicating that they, too, saw the difference in the boy. There was no discussion, just the hope that he, like Tiger, would snap back to his old self in time.

Having gotten them a few steps ahead, the Freemans' friends returned to Madison and summer wore on. With help they had planted more corn than ever. Now it was time to harvest which took Moses and Solomon working steadily all day every day to get done. Lela neglected all non-essential tasks like mending and sewing so she could feed the stock. That allowed the men a little more time with the harvest. Young as she was, Sarah helped her mother tend the kitchen garden, keep clothes washed, and put out two meals a day.

The exhausted couple lay in bed after an especially grueling day. "Moses?" Lela whispered. His low grunt told her he was listening. "You and Solomon are working so hard, I worry for you."

"Can't be helped, Lela."

"Moses, do you see something in Solomon since he got home? Something quiet and dark?" Lela asked in a whisper as she placed her hand on her husband's arm.

His big rough hand covered hers. "Uh-huh. Can't put a name to it but it there. Don't reckon we ever know 'xactly what happen when he gone."

"I'm afraid I don't really want to know. Is that bad, Moses?"

"Ain't nothin' in the world bad 'bout a mama not wantin' to hear her chile's sufferin'." With a deep, tired breath Moses sighed. "We just keep on like we always do, Lela. He know how we feel and we do anything for him. But he growin' up and we got to let him have his own feelin's – even the hard ones." Cradling her in his arms he said, "Now, wife, you rest yourself. That boy gon' be jus' fine . . ."

"I pray so, Moses, I do pray so."

CHAPTER FIFTEEN

August, 1871 -- Lela stepped off the front porch of the bunk house, raising a hand to shade her eyes from the sun. Little Sarah was rocking her beautiful doll who nobody, including herself, touched before washing hands thoroughly. "Mercy, Sarah, it's hot already. And I thought your brother would be in from the field before now."

Mimicking her mother, Sarah, exclaimed, "Mercy, mercy, mercy!" Lela turned and laughed at her darling daughter.

"Come with me, Apple of My Eye, and let's get those chickens in their house before night brings the foxes."

"Bad foxes," Sarah chattered as she ran into the house to put her baby to bed. Hand in hand mother and daughter got a pan of corn from the barn and started calling, almost singing, "Here chick, chick! Chicky come here!" Sarah's job was to sprinkle her small handfuls of the gold sparsely along their path to lure the chickens into the chicken yard. Creatures of habit, the chickens knew that if they responded to that song they would be rewarded with a nice corn supper. Then Lela would sow a bit more corn to lead them into the house where they roosted for the night.

"Do they like their house, Mama?" the inquisitive little girl asked.

"Oh, I believe they do, Sarah. Maybe they know it helps keep them safe." Never missing an opportunity for a new lesson or emphasis on an old one, Lela continued. "Remember, baby, we must always be sure that all the hens are in their house and put the board down on its door to keep them safe."

Sarah had heard this part before. "Yes ma'am, and check the wire on the yard to be sure there ain't – uh, there aren't – any holes where Mr. Fox can get in."

"Exactly, right, Sarah. You know so much you'll be in charge of the chickens soon." The little one basked in the compliment from her mother who posed a question. "And what's the last thing we do as we put the chickens to bed?" Mother and daughter had been so deep in their poultry lesson that they didn't notice that Solomon had come up. He leaned against the barn watching.

The girl's brow wrinkled in thought. "Mmmm . . . oh! Lock the latch on the door to the chicken yard!"

Swooping her up from behind and raising her above his head, Solomon said, "Yes ma'am Missy Sarah. We have to do everything we can to keep Mr. Fox and his friends out of the chickens." She squealed in delight as he lowered her to his waist. "Tiger can't do all the work around here; we have to do our part, too."

Lela loved the easy affection Solomon showed Sarah as much as she loved the way Sarah idolized her big brother. Sometimes she thought his moments with Sarah were his only untroubled times. "Son, do you suppose that Sarah will be able to gather the eggs in the morning on her own?"

"Could I, Mama? Could I really?" Sarah squealed. "I'll leave the pen gate hooked open and put out their breakfast corn and won't break an egg. Not even one," the girl chattered. Before Lela could even answer, Sarah let out a shriek and cried, "Daddy! Daddy!" She ran into Moses' arms and clung to him without noticing he wasn't squeezing her back quite as hard as usual.

Lela and Solomon looked at each other in concern and rushed to greet Moses. Solomon took Sarah to ease his father's arms and Lela laid a hand on his shoulder. "Moses?" she whispered. His look told her they would discuss things later once Sarah was abed. That was excuse enough for the short term, but he well knew that the discussion would wait not a minute after that.

Sarah was tucked in early, and the three older Freemans sat around the fire. "Took you a mite longer to get to Newnansville and back this time, Papa." Solomon's eyes caught his father's. "You alright?" The rest of the question lingered.

Just as Lela opened her mouth Moses held up his hand and said, "I'm fine. I'm just fine." Looking from son to wife and back to son again he couldn't contain a grin, even if it did hurt to smile. "It did take a little longer than I 'spected but I'm home and safe." He paused dramatically and reached into his jacket as he stood. Revealing a folded paper with a flourish, he announced with all the formality he could muster, "We got us a patent land deed – official and legal-like!"

After a moment's pause, the three moved together in celebration. "I'll say they was some there didn't want me to have a deed, they surely was. Didn't seem to matter we had our proof of homesteading and were due a deed, they just didn't like it."

Lela looked up at her husband, her eyes squinted and mouth clinched in a crooked warning. Moses knew that face showed there was more to tell. He also knew he only wanted Lela to know the victory. "That's really about all there was. I was polite and patient as could be and there was them didn't want me to get home with it, but here I am and we got something big to celebrate!"

Lela and Solomon both knew that Moses' errand had taken so long because he took time to work the worst of the damage off his face and body. He did that for their benefit but she wished he would open up and tell her the real story -- the whole story. She also knew that if he ever told it to anyone it would be Solomon and that she was destined to know no more than the happy fact that they were now in full legal ownership of eighty acres. *The Freeman Farm free and clear. What a nice sound that has.*

CHAPTER SIXTEEN

December, 1871 – Summer turned to fall and melted into winter with hardly a notice. The place was running on pure habit and determination. Lela worried that far too many chores were heaped onto Sarah, but there seemed little alternative. At least for most of them, they were together so lessons in counting and letters could continue.

They had never had the means for lavish celebration, but Christmas at the Freemans' had always been special. This year it was wrapped in disquiet. Solomon brought Granny Ma from town and she and Lela prepared a special meal featuring smoked ham. The sugar and flour Solomon picked up at Mr. Hart's gave the ladies a rare chance to make a tender sugar cake instead of their usual coarse corn cakes.

Small gifts were exchanged each a demonstration of special thought to its creation for the receiver. Little Sarah had nothing in her memory to compare this observance to and was the logical center of attention so she had a grand time.

Since returning from the Groaton place and seeing his father's injuries from the trip to Newnansville, Solomon worked more and spoke less. He wasn't mean or disrespectful, but kept his own counsel. Watching Granny Ma watch Solomon, Lela sought the older woman for advice.

"Granny, you see it, don't you?"

"Hmm, hmm, hmm," was all that came from the woman's slowly shaking head.

"What is it, Granny?" Lela pressed. "What is it you see?" Lela responded to Granny's silence with something she recalled. "Solomon and I had a strange talk about people – women in particular -- who seem friendly at one time but distant another. I asked a couple of questions without being too nosey and finally suggested that at those monthly times a woman just doesn't come out with people much. I've missed some of the talks we should have had when he was younger but he understands now." Lela posed a curious thought. "Granny, do you suppose he's met a girl someplace?"

Granny sat heavily on a bench, shook her head, and tried to put her thoughts into words. "Ain't sure, Baby. Be like they's a cloud around that boy – a heavy, dark one."

Lela understood exactly what Granny meant. The two spoke in hushed whispers as Solomon left the mule lot on Sally. When he wasn't working Solomon was rarely found near the farmstead. Always one to ramble and explore, the young man seemed, more than ever, to need what was hidden in the woods.

In idle consciousness Solomon let Old Sally make the way, ambling this way and that through the tangled woods. The December chill had left heavy dew, not quite frozen, on the pine boughs so when Solomon looked upward he saw jewels made by the new day's sun. Occasionally they entered a portion of virgin forest where the sun barely reached the ground through the soaring dense pines and Sally's steps made no sound on the carpet of fallen needles. It suited her rider that Sally couldn't move so quickly any more as he fell easily into her plodding rhythm allowing them both to breathe deeply and clear their cobwebs – from her body and from his troubled mind.

Solomon, unable to stop the tumble of images in his mind, didn't note the rustle to his right. Her hearing about like most old bodies, Sally didn't hear it either. True to her lifelong habit she jumped straight-legged to a stop when she sensed something amiss. Drifting Solomon wobbled on the blanketed seat and shook his head to attention. Sally looked right and nervously stepped left, feeling but not seeing danger.

The low, gruff snort from behind a little scrub blind was familiar. *Same bad just keep comin' back to us, Sally.* The boy wasn't sure whether he had thought it or said it but there wasn't time to wonder.

Out from the thicket lumbered an odd looking brindle bull with miss-matched horns. Keeping Sally calm, Solomon faced the beast and looked right into the eyes on either side of a big, hairless slash at the top of his face. "What you want with us. Ain't no way you know it me." The bull snorted a response. "Well, you meaner 'n ever it look like. Now, you go on and we go the other way."

As Solomon turned Sally to leave in as fast a trot as she could manage, the bull lunged like a shot covering the space between them before they had a chance. Long accustomed to his left horn being useless in a fight, the monster expertly lowered his head and rammed into Sally thrusting the upturned right horn into the mule's chest and pushing. Solomon barely cleared his leg from part of the crush and the force of the bull knocked him off Sally's back where he landed in a daze. Shaking his senses back he could see the bull move more quickly than he had thought possible, pulling out and goring the crying mule again until she fell over.

Solomon jumped up, whip in hand and said some of the words he had learned in Cedar Key. There was no saving Sally but he was bound to punish the bull. Not considering that the bull could do him exactly what he had done to Sally, only worse, Solomon stepped toward the killer yelling and reaching to his side. As he approached the beast from behind he used a side to side action that allowed him to welt the bull back and forth with every swing of his long whip. He got in several strikes before the bull turned from Sally.

As in a trance, Solomon continued to assault the bull cutting across the old scar on his face. The bull didn't turn away but the constant barrage kept him from continuing his charge. A direct hit across his right eye gushed blood and the bull bellowed, his eye nearly drawn from its socket. Confused through the red veil, the brindle staggered away quickly learning to angle his head to the right to make his way.

Solomon could do nothing to save Sally but he sat by the faithful old mule stroking her head and telling her how much she had helped the Freemans make a success of their farm. He knew they'd never have gotten their deed without her. "Good old girl, you are, Sally. Don't know what Sudie'll do without you." Tears streaming, he said, "Don't know what I'll do without you either." She didn't appear to be in much pain. Her life was just flowing from her in a steady stream of blood. At his final good-bye, Solomon's jaw set and he vowed revenge on the animal.

Aside from the fact that the place couldn't operate without mules, there were three reasons Solomon went to New Troy to buy two new mules the day after Sally's death – he still had a little cash left from the bonus Pete gave him from the drive, old Sudie's working days were about over, and he felt responsible for Sally's death. Solomon left for New Town having warned his parents and Granny Ma that he would be back within the week with the mules and supplies on Lela's list.

The household was relieved that it didn't take the whole week for Solomon to return. Skillfully packed on the new mules, the result of Solomon's woods ramble included a deer, several rabbits, backstrap and roasts butchered from another red meat animal, and a mysterious multi-colored tail that remained hidden from his family.

After Sally's death, which Solomon saw as murder, he would be on the alert and knew he would eventually encounter his old enemy. His next meeting with the bull had come much sooner than he'd expected, which worked in the young hunter's favor. The pain of the attack was still fresh and raw, fueling his final vengeance. Keeping only the choicest cuts, the bulk of the meat and hide were left to waste in the woods where the demon had spent his entire ill- tempered life.

Always glad for fresh meat, Lela met her son to take the small game while Moses helped him skin out the deer and put the other meat in the smoke house. The weather was chilly so there was little wasted meat. Granny Ma sat near the cook pot trimming turnip roots and onion for rabbit stew and noted the struggle in Lela's face. Lela turned to her dear friend and explained, "I read the Bible last night; even great Moses felt over-burdened. It sounded so much like Solomon. 'I am not able to bear all these people alone, because the burden is too heavy for me.'"

Old and sage, Granny Ma let Lela take her time until the young mother finally asked, "Granny, am I seeing straight? Do you see such despair in his face?"

"Mmmm hummm." Granny replied in long syllables. "Right plain to them that looks."

"What do you suppose happened out there?"

"No tellin', baby. Jes ain't no tellin'." Granny Ma groaned as she leaned to dump the vegetables into the pot. "Baby, he gettin' out on his own 'n ain't nothing you can do to stop it. He want you to know what troublin' him, he tell you. Elsewise best to leave it be."

"I know that, Granny, truly I do. It's just so hard to watch him suffer and know that he doesn't feel he can lean on me. He just seems so hardened."

"Tha's what churrin' do, baby. They take all you teach 'em and start keepin' they own counsel." Granny rubbed her aching back. "That boy got lots of new feelin's bubblin' up and gon' have to figure it all out; what parts he tell you and them he don't. He gone through some evil in his short years, specially these late ones; might be he trying to protect you much as you want to protect him." Taking a final deep breath, Granny Ma finished her speech. "What you got to do, Lela, is hold strong for him. Don't let him see into your worryin' heart 'bout this."

Lela searched the wise woman for more answers but knew there were none. "I'll try, Granny, most truly I'll try."

---

[1] Numbers 11:14

CHAPTER SEVENTEEN

Thanks to the aide of Pete and his men, the planting and other spring chores were nearly caught up but there was still plenty to do. Now that the fields and garden were up and growing they had to be tended: fertilized, watered when possible, staked when necessary, and weeded. Solomon had always been the one with itchy feet, but this time it was Moses who became restless and fidgety. Lela watched and held her tongue for several days. Finally, after noticing how frantically Moses worked every day she became concerned for him. "Moses," she asked, "do you feel alright?"

"Shore, Lela honey," he replied. "Just tryin' to get a little ahead's all."

"Moses Freeman," his wife said with authority that contradicted her petite stature, "you aren't acting yourself and you know it. Now, are you going to tell me what's making you like that spinning top Solomon brought to Sarah?"

Moses tried to avoid a direct answer but finally he responded. "Reckon maybe I got little more of Solomon's restlessness in me than I thought. Just feel like I got to get done what I can while I can."

"You've always done that, Moses. And you've never taken time off from it." Lela made sure she had her husband's full attention. "Why don't you try doing what Solomon does and take a break once in a while? It might restore you some."

"It's alright, Lela. Something will come up soon for a rest. Just now I gotta do it all while I can." He stood straighter and walked back toward the barn and Lela was left wishing she could reach her husband more effectively sometimes.

Spring came and went leaving fields and gardens producing well and making more work than ever. Moses said it was a double-edge sword; the farm was legally theirs and they had put more acres in use each year. But all four Freemans were on the verge of exhaustion trying to manage a farm that had grown beyond their manpower. Even having Granny Ma with them for longer periods of time was a pleasure and a help but not enough.

Lela had just sat under the shade of an oak tree to shell black-eyed peas when Pete Harker galloped into the yard and bounded off Diamond's back. "Hello to you, Mrs. Freeman!" he shouted as he led his horse to the trough for a drink.

Quickly setting down her work, she ran toward Pete only to be upstaged by Sarah. "Mr. Pete! Mr. Pete! Swing, Mr. Pete!" the little girl sang.

With a big laugh Mr. Pete did just that, swinging her around and around. "There you are pretty girl. You can fly like a bird." Setting Sarah gently on her feet before he got dizzy, Pete turned toward Lela.

"Look at you," she said. "That's a stylish suit of clothes, Pete. I've never seen you in such before." She tentatively touched the sleeve of his coat, relishing the feel of fabric quality she'd not felt in over five years. "What's the occasion, Pete?"

"An occasion it is, Lela. I have some surprises for you." Pete's eyes glowed like Lela had never seen them and he was jittery, looking all around the yard. "Where are Moses and Solomon?" he asked anxiously.

"They're probably still in the corn field, Pete. There's lots of day left, you know." She stooped to pick up a skillet and started banging as hard as she could with a big spoon.

Sarah's fingers went directly into her ears – she had heard the sound before. "This should bring them in," she said. "Probably in a panic," she laughed.

Sure enough, Moses and Solomon tore into the yard, their faces painted with fear. Moses pulled up short and slid off Belle's back. Blowing hard from exertion he gasped, "Lord a mighty, I thought there was somethin' big happenin'." Extending his hand to Pete, he laughed, "Ain't nothin' but you, Pete." Noticing his friend's appearance, "And look at you anyway, Pete. Ain't never seed such a figure."

By the time they had greeted Pete, a large, slow moving figure appeared in the doorway of the bunk house. One hand leaning heavily on a rough hewn walking stick and the other at her heart, Granny Ma shouted, "Ohhhhh, Mr. Pete Harker, jes' look at you!"

Pete strode to the porch and helped the elderly woman down the step to the ground and gave her a big kiss on the check sending her into a fit of school girl giggling. "Granny Ma! What a wonderful surprise. It's perfect – the whole family is here now."

"Not quite all," Pete muttered under a smile.

Granny was settled comfortably onto a large stump that Solomon had carved into a chair, breathing hard but still grinning and chuckling. It had been months since the Freemans had seen their friend from Madison County so questions and answers flew quickly.

Finally, Lela put her hands on her hips and got to the real question of the day. "Now, Pete, what are you doing riding into the woods in such fine clothes? Was I your wife I'd thrash you with the broom for the chance of spoiling such duds."

"I'll just bet you would, too, Lela." Looking toward Moses sternly, Pete teased, "There's your warning, Moses. Don't stretch your limits with this little lady!"

Before Moses could assure Pete that he was well aware of Lela's authority, the increasing rumble of approaching wagons was heard. Pete grinned more broadly than they'd ever seen and Solomon voiced everyone's question, "What in the world . . . ?"

There were two wagons along with Slim, Manuel, and Charlie as outriders. Both wagons were packed tightly and covered with canvas and next to the driver of the first wagon sat a delicate figure in an unadorned but elegant dress. Slim dismounted to help the lady, for surely this was a lady of the first degree, down from the wagon then stepped to the second wagon and lifted a small boy down. Unnerved in such unfamiliar surroundings, the child ran to clutch at the woman's skirt

Pete knew the instant it happened. The lady stopped about half way across the yard and Lela's eyes blinked and squinted as though she couldn't see clearly. "Pete?" she gasped. Her voice was almost inaudible.

Pete's single word sounded like silk. "Yes." By the time the two women embraced each other Moses and Pete were grinning broadly and Solomon and Granny Ma were shaking their heads in confusion and astonishment. The little boy stood aside in the fear of the unknown.

Moses stepped to Pete, slapping him hard on the back and shaking his hand. "You sly dog, Pete. Lela said last time you's here somethin' was going on with you. Never onct would guess it be this."

"By the time I figured the whole thing out, Moses," Pete explained, "I was so smitten there was no turning back. Then I just thought it would make a good surprise for both of them." They moved toward their wives, one milky and blond and the other with skin of coffee with milk stirred in. They turned toward the men and, the truth was unmistakable. There was a general resemblance, but they had identical exotically almond-shaped green eyes.

Moses automatically moved to the visitor and extended his hand. "'Gradlations, Mrs. Harker!"

Mrs. Harker paused just long enough for Moses to feel her hesitation then she gave Moses a most lady-like hand shake. "Moses," she said shocked at his burn-scarred face, "how good to see you again."

Pushing right through her coolness, he said, "Welcome to our place. Anytime you here, it your place, too, just like it is for Pete."

"Why, thank you, Moses." She glanced behind Moses and cocked her head in concentration. "Solomon? Lela can this strapping boy be Solomon?"

Lela laughed proudly. "Yes, Betsy, that handsome boy is my Solomon." Motioning for Solomon to step forward she made introductions, "Son, you don't recognize her after so long but this is Miss Elizabeth – Betsy."

"And this is my little boy, Richard Edward Stimes," Betsy announced proudly as the boy peeked around his mother to inspect the alien faces. And he was confused. He had never seen white people and coloreds so friendly. He was only five, but he knew it didn't feel normal somehow.

Nodding with friendly respect Solomon welcomed her. "Miss . . . Miss Betsy, you and Mama make reverse images like two halves." Stunned at his immediate perception, they said nothing. "That means I have," Solomon said with thoughtful wonder and a slowly emerging smile, "I have an aunt."

Pete stepped in to mask the discomfort he saw in Betsy and the defense he felt in Moses and Lela. "So," he drawled dramatically, "Elizabeth? Lela? How do you like your surprise?"

Pete's bride turned on him and spoke more shrilly than necessary. "Pete Harker, what possessed you to pull a stunt like this? I dare say we both deserved some warning!" Surprise set on Pete's face and froze his mouth.

There'd been no time to anticipate all of the possibilities of their reunion, but Lela wasn't surprised that Betsy's response wasn't altogether welcoming. She'd always used humor to diffuse Betsy before. She hoped it would still work. "Land sakes, Betsy," Lela laughed as she took Betsy's hand, "if we'd had warning we'd both have just stirred in circles like mad crows. No, it's much more fun this way!"

The awkward moment passed and the rest of the afternoon and evening were spent unloading wagons, reminiscing, and getting acquainted. Pete, Betsy, and Richard moved into the bunk side of the bunk house, leaving the Freemans in their now-accustomed living quarters. The hands camped under the trees, retreating to the canvas-covered wagons when showers came.

Their story unfolded answering Lela's questions. Betsy's husband, Mr. Stimes, was a member of the Atlanta aristocracy. Before the war he managed, according to rumor through evasion of military service and black market dealing, several small business ventures. He and Betsy met and married after a whirlwind courtship when she arrived in Atlanta shortly after the Freemans left Georgia, her father's death, and the rock bottom sale of Hill's Run. Betsy confided to Lela, "I had barely enough money to live with friends for a few months. I needed security and he needed a hostess with a pretty face and social graces."

Lela's heart broke for the pain she saw in Betsy's eyes and knew the story had a bad ending. After a few months Stimes, plummeting after the loss of his assets, went into a warehouse he was to turn over the next day and hung himself. Lela knew nothing to do but hold Betsy's hands tightly and listen. "He didn't even know that I was with child," she said weakly. "Maybe that would have made some difference."

Ultimately, Betsy found a place in the home of old family friends in Savannah. Suffering far less damage than Atlanta, it was much more revived and prosperous than the ravaged Atlanta. She was to be teacher for their three children while she awaited the birth of her child. As a member of the household and relative of a prominent Savannah family, Betsy resumed a minimal role in society. Because she was an employee trading her instruction for room and board for herself and Richard, when he was born, she was on the outside of the inner circles in which she had grown up. It was an odd existence in limbo. Not unpleasant, but not entirely comfortable or suitable for a young woman of her birth and genteel breeding.

Day-by-day the Harkers' saga wove through the routine – cooking, washing, tending animals and crops. Lela was pleased but surprised that Betsy would actually help feed chickens and hang out wash. Circumstances had surely changed her because she'd certainly never done such on Hill's Run.

Once the hands returned to Madison, the three men worked the fields, and Moses and Solomon learned the story from Pete's perspective. It was impossible to do much talking while they worked, but the Freeman men questioned Pete during every water break until they felt they knew the whole story. They knew Pete had sought backing for the bank he wanted to open in Madison. They didn't know what a risk he was taking because there was no structure for chartered banks in Florida. Pete's would be a private bank which meant he provided the securities for its operation and assumed the risk for its failure. Wishing him well with the venture was about the only connection they had to the intricacies of the investment and banking world.

Late one afternoon they took the long way back to the house, both mules and men relishing the cool of the river. Sitting in the sun Pete's faraway look matched his miracle story. "When I learned that a couple of old friends of my father's were in Savannah I knew that was my only real hope of connecting to enough investors to open the bank."

"Must take a powerful lot of money to have a bank, Pete," Solomon observed solemnly.

"More than I had, that's sure," replied Pete. He fell into his story and seemed unable to stop. "One Saturday night I attended another fancy dinner that I knew was a test of my value to do business with this group. Nobody would invest in my bank unless I could pass inspection socially. I really think it was mostly to drag out the discussions to see how persistent I could be."

"The habit of making a slightly late and mostly grand entrance never caught on with me, so I arrived right on time and entered quietly. I stopped in the doorway to give the butler my hat and gloves and looked into the house to get my bearings, having never been there before." His head slowly shook back and forth, as though still in disbelief, and Pete's story continued. "Floating down the stairs was a young woman in a pale green dress. She was tiny, almost frail, and she was so graceful that it looked like her feet didn't even touch the carpeted steps."

"Must have been a sight to see, Pete," inserted Moses. Moses didn't even think Pete heard him. It didn't matter. Moses, Solomon, and Lela had spent several days now guessing how in the world Pete and Betsy had crossed paths. The last they'd heard she was in Atlanta.

"She didn't see me. I don't think she really saw anybody." As though trying to solve a mystery, Pete's face tensed. "She spoke with people and was pleasant but not open. I don't think she cared whether she was there or not."

Pete's story went on, "I couldn't help but look for her across the rooms throughout the night and quickly resented having to talk business after dinner when all I wanted to do was ask her to dance just so I could talk with her." Shifting to ease his troublesome hip, Pete went on. "Afraid the night would run out before I at least found out who she was, I asked one of my prospective investors. I nearly coughed out a sip of good bourbon when he told me she was, though not actually related, part of his household."

Pete chuckled as he said, "I must have been pretty transparent because he told me her name – Mrs. Elizabeth Stimes, a widow much too young – and encouraged me to ask her to dance. Now I'd not danced since before the war and wasn't in any hurry to demonstrate how stiff and clumsy I was at it, but I just had to meet that woman."

"So, she danced with you, Pete?"   Solomon whispered, afraid to break the moment but having to know.

"Oh, she danced with me, Solomon, such as the dancing was. It didn't take long for her to see that dancing wasn't the safest way to become acquainted with me if she wanted to keep those little feet of hers attached!" The men stood to gather the animals and head back to the house. "In short, we spent a great deal of time together for the next few days – just as much as I could convince her to. I heard her story and she heard mine. I met her son." Pete paused, contemplating the mystery, then continued. "She felt responsible to her benefactor and neither of us wanted to be impulsive but it only took a few months and a couple more visits to Savannah for me to convince her that she and Richard should be in Madison with me."

Solomon made the connection. "That's why we ain't seen you since last fall, Pete." Harker nodded like a boy caught sneaking cookies.

"Well, we glad she weren't so stubborn as she was as a girl, Pete, or you'd never got her to Madison," Moses observed.

"Oh, no," Pete admitted, "she is most definitely not over that stubborn streak, Moses. It comes out right regularly!"

"But, Pete," Solomon asked thoughtfully, "how come you didn't know her name?"

"That's part of the mystery, son," Pete explained. "I don't know that I'd actually ever heard her married name and Lela only called her Betsy. What I don't understand is how I could have missed the resemblance between Betsy and Lela. I'll never understand that!"

"Well, you must have," Solomon said sensibly, "or you wouldn't have thought to give them such a surprise."

"It was that last trip here that I saw it. By then I knew I was going to marry Betsy and didn't want to spoil things by telling too soon. I guess what they say is true – love is blind!" They all laughed but Solomon wasn't sure he understood what was so funny.

The ride from New Troy was quiet. Too quiet for comfort. With Lela and Betsy in the wagon and Moses driving and Pete on horseback, the morning had begun with high spirits. Betsy had joined Pete on two previous trips to the Freemans' and seemed to enjoy her time with Lela. She certainly preferred her more comfortable life in Madison, though it wasn't at all like Savannah or Atlanta. Nevertheless, she had been surprisingly sporting about the rustic life in the country. She hadn't been keen on Solomon staying home with Sarah and Richard – partly because she felt Richard wasn't cut out for rough country life -- but Pete assured her that the children would be fine. Besides, Granny Ma was there and what he thought but did not say was that he thought that a little dirt would be good for the boy.

From the moment Betsy saw tiny New Troy, though, Lela knew they were in for a day of it. Compared to what she was used to, Mr. Hart's store was pitiful and she sniffed in disdain for the few other small shops and their limited wares. "Betsy," Pete admonished quietly, "this isn't Savannah and will never be. There are a few things we need and this is a treat for Lela and Moses."

Pete had seen her haughty side. He knew it was bred into her, but it was unattractive and could be barbed. When Betsy thrust her parcels into Lela's arms commandingly, Pete gallantly took both their purchases and Betsy's arm and headed for the wagon. He hoped Lela hadn't felt what he had seen, but in his heart knew that she was very aware of it.

After quickly stowing the purchases Pete turned to his wife. "Betsy, I've not taken to telling you what to do and don't plan to. We're both adults and shouldn't need such." Betsy's face showed that she had no idea why Pete was upset, but he obviously was. "But, I'm telling you today that if I ever see you disrespect the Freemans like that again, you'll regret it." Lowering his voice to insure they weren't overheard he continued, "She's not your slave. Not ever again. My God, woman, Lela is your sister!"

"Pete," Betsy began, "I didn't think. It was just the natural thing to do." A little too impetuously she asked, "Anyway, what will people think?"

"I don't much care what people think and as little as you obviously think of New Troy and its citizens, I can't think why you would care either." Glancing at the waiting Freemans, Pete tried to get things settled quickly and quietly so there'd be no more discord. "I know that you were raised playing one role while Lela played another. And, for their protection, I realize we have to watch appearances. The last thing I want is to have Lela and Moses hurt or embarrassed."

"Is that all you think of, Pete Harker?" Betsy shot back. "Protecting your precious friends?"

While his words may not have, Pete's smoldering look got Betsy's attention. "The Freemans are my friends, the best I have. They've saved my life, we've done business together, and I trust them with my life. That means I trust the two most precious things in my life – you and Richard -- to them, too. I love you Betsy but, make no mistake, it won't go well if you can't control your high and mighty attitude."

His wife opened and closed her mouth like a hungry fish for a few seconds, hardened her face, and took a deep breath. "Alright, Pete," she said through clinched teeth. "I've always loved Lela and like Moses and Solomon. Things are just different now."

"You're right," Pete said gentling his tone somewhat. "We have all had to adjust to it, but we aren't in the old world now and I expect you to remember that in word and deed." Betsy swallowed hard and nodded, but didn't speak. "Now," Pete said brightly, "it's my intention that the rest of the day go well for all of us and a lot of that depends upon you." He offered his arm to his wife and escorted her toward the Freemans.

"Everybody ready to give that new boarding house a try? I'm starved," Pete announced as they approached Lela and Moses. His friends looked suspiciously at him and he felt Betsy's hand clinch on his arm. He cast a warning glance at Betsy, and smiled at the Freemans. "There's no reason why this can't work." And into the boarding house they went.

New Troy's new boarding house also served meals to the public and made quite an addition to the town. The owner was so shocked at the entrance of the two couples that she didn't think quickly enough to object to their being seated. If she didn't object to that she could hardly refuse to serve them food. The four fell into a slightly altered relationship to avoid trouble. The Freemans didn't appear to be the Harkers' equals. They were more like hired servants.

The two couples turned heads causing tongues to wag and a few muttered slurs but the day went fairly smoothly overall. The quiet ride home was hard to define. There was no overt anger or embarrassment nor was there the normal excitement of a trip to town. Each of the four seemed caught in contemplation and assessment, most of which would probably never be discussed openly. Times were surely different and hard to navigate.

Several days later, as the Harkers prepared to return to Madison, Pete had the opportunity he'd sought to speak with Lela. He was confident that Lela knew he didn't share Betsy's remnant attitudes but wanted to assure her that he would do all he could to help her see them as equals. Had he thought clearly enough he would have known he needn't have worried.

Lela did the reassuring. "Pete Harker, you are an old softy and a sweetheart," she said patting his hand as she would a small child. "I know exactly what Betsy is feeling. I have spent most of my life living between two worlds. When I was with Betsy, I was almost a lady, but always in the background. In the quarters I was a slave, but was seen as different, arrogant, better than. Finally, when Moses and I made our home, at least when we were in our house, I discovered myself – no torn loyalties, no narrowed eyes or whispers. Being here – in our very own home – I have found myself and I don't intend to lose that for anyone."

Pete's relief was clear. Lela continued. "I understand that we are still in lives of two worlds and we've all had to adjust. Betsy will have to move past what she has known her whole life and, because she has rarely had to adjust to anything, it isn't as easy as it might be for us." Pete started to speak but Lela hushed him. "Yes, Pete, I feel the strain sometimes – the snobbery, the tendency to see me as a servant. But I also know that, in her own way and as much as she knows how, Betsy loves me. What she knows and now has to acknowledge is splitting her into pieces and we have to give her time and encouragement to pull herself into the world as we know it."

Shaking his head in amazement, Pete whispered, "Lela Freeman, how did you become so very wise?" Her rich green eyes were filled with thanks for his worry and assurance that she would be alright. "I should have known that you'd be the one to counsel and comfort me."

CHAPTER EIGHTEEN

With summer came the unending toil of harvest time. The men cropped, cut, picked, dried and stored, and renewed for fall planting. The women cut, peeled, or shelled and preserved and stored the food stuffs. Even little Sarah had to learn chores, though she was still at an age when it was all so new that it was a game she cheerfully joined. She was a hard little worker, though, and learned quickly. Lela knew she would be a big help as she got just a little older.

Summer and early fall were always long, hard, broiling days and the fact that much of the food preservation required time over the cook fire didn't help. But, their labors were fruitful and they had a storeroom full of the garden's and fields' bounties. Once the season changed, meat could be hunted and put in the smokehouse and winter nourishment would be assured. They were surely in better position than they were five years before when food was scarce in every season.

Throughout the summer, when anyone went to town, the most recent newspaper was brought home from Mr. Hart's. Moses, never the reader that Lela and Solomon were, labored over the news of the coming elections in November and encouraged them to read aloud. This insured that he had read correctly and that they were both informed about the upcoming vote. Moses was determined to vote in the presidential election and asked Mr. Hart questions about the polling place, process, and anything else he could think of to ask. Despite a nagging foreboding, Mr. Hart tried to answer all of Moses' questions.

October, 1872 -- The headline on the counter matched the talk that swirled through the region about the big voting time coming up soon. Solomon asked Mr. Hart for details and clarification.

"Date is set for Monday, two weeks hence, Solomon," explained the shopkeeper. He went on as he passed the small document printed on dusty colored paper to Solomon. "This ain't rightly news any more but you'll find the rules and what's to be voted on in it." Hart returned to his ledger confident that the boy didn't need his help. In fact, he was fairly sure that Solomon Freeman could read better than he could.

Solomon finished reading, folded the paper, and leaned on the counter. "Mr. Hart, Papa says since emancipation voting marked a free man." The young man squinted as he read the tiny print. Says here, "Amendment Fifteen ratified in February allows that the 'right to vote shall not be denied or abridged on the basis of race, color or previous condition of servitude.' That means every man can vote and I believe my daddy would sure like to vote." He looked to Hart for affirmation.

Hart had learned, despite his initial resistance, that these Freemans were decent, solid people. But voting was delicate territory. "I can see his point, Solomon, I surely can."

Solomon felt more than heard hesitation in Hart's voice. "Do you think it's a bad idea, Mr. Hart?"

"Oh, no, don't mistake me. I don't know . . ." Hart hesitated. "Know you got to be of age, own property . . ." His voice drifted off.

"I don't even know what of age is," Solomon jested, "but I 'magine Papa's got there by now." Mr. Hart was relieved he hadn't angered the boy – yet, at least. Solomon continued. "We got the deed alright. Paper here says got to read and write."

"I don't know all the rules, but Moses reads, doesn't he?" the merchant asked.

"Yes sir. Not so good, but he reads and writes enough to make out I'd say." The little bell over the door clanged so Solomon stepped aside to inspect the knives on display. When the customer left he returned to the counter and faced Mr. Hart squarely.

He didn't feel at all threatened but Hart knew that the discussion was turning serious. It didn't help that, with the store being the largest business in town and the post office to boot, people expected him to know what was going on in the world beyond Lafayette County. "You know more, Mr. Hart, and you aren't tellin' it." Solomon's voice was calm

Steeling himself T. C. Hart spoke directly. "I'm talkin' man-to-man here, Solomon, don't mean disrespect." Solomon nodded. "I'm plannin' to vote myself and hope others will, too. I'm not easy about it, though, I got to tell you." Hart made a few nervous swipes at the dust that had settled on the checker board. "I don't know who'll be in charge – whether it be folks from here or outsiders. Don't matter much." Solomon could tell Mr. Hart was struggling to have his say. "Most 'round here ain't got to know you like I have. Might be they don't let Moses vote."

"Yes, sir, I reckon that might be. But we got freedom papers and deed. Seems they 'bout have to 'llow it." Pointing to the newspaper he added, "Says here this number fifteen makes it law."

"Seems so," Hart agreed, "but you know y'all and Granny Ma 'bout the only of your people right near and folks hold on to their opinions of things mighty hard."

Solomon asked directly, "Mr. Hart, do **you** think my Papa shouldn't be allowed to vote?"

This was a test for T. R. Hart and he knew that Solomon would know if he didn't tell the full truth. "Solomon, when your family walked into this store that first time I was set and bound to tell you, you couldn't stay."

Hart timidly continued, "That you'd have to find some other place to get your supplies. I was ready to say that even knowing that there wasn't another place near and even if there was they'd tell you the same thing."

"But that's not what you did."

"No, greatly to my own surprise, that's not what I did." Hart closed the ledger book and put his hand flat on it. "This here ledger is full of accounts late paid, way behind, some I know never be paid."

"Didn't never think about that. Must be hard doing business with folks you know ain't payin'."

"That's a fact, son, and prices up most I've ever seen for everything making it harder still even for them who want to pay." Hart shook his head sadly then leaned across the counter toward Solomon. "But that ain't the point I'm making. There's a page in that ledger with Freeman at the top and you won't find anything but paid in full. Can't say that about many."

"Papa believe in payin' his way."

"I know he does and everybody who does business with him appreciates that – even them that won't admit to it right out. Point is, Solomon, I was prepared to hate the Freemans and anybody else like you. There's them says taking your money is one thing but being over friendly is another." It seemed a dam had burst in Mr. Hart and, once started, he couldn't stop the words.

"I'll be honest with you, Solomon. Had Pete Harker not been with you that first day I'd just as like to have turned you around and sent you out. But Harker doesn't pay your bills or work your place or live honest for you. You do those things for yourselves. I come to see the Freemans as people and that ain't been my usual view."

"I understand what you're sayin', Mr. Hart, and I know Papa and Mama would thank you just like I do."

"We can both read what the law says, but this is a long way from Washington and all those big decisions. I just got a bad feeling and hate to see your Papa be refused at the voting," Hart said firmly.

"I tell him, Mr. Hart, and thank you for the warning. I'll take this paper if it's alright with you. We read it over good – Mama be sure of that. Then Papa decide for himself."

By the time election day arrived the Freemans had studied and debated the voting process and issues up for voting. Moses stuck to the principle that it was voting that made a man a true citizen. He started early, washed and dressed the very best he could, carefully stowed his emancipation papers and the patent deed in the inside pocket of his coat, and proudly headed to New Troy to vote for his very first time.

When he returned home late that afternoon he sat so straight and proud on the new mule that he almost masked the cut on his mouth and the tenderness in his side and back.

"Moses!" an alarmed Lela said as she helped him from the mule. "You're hurt! I'm so sorry it didn't go like you'd hoped."

His smile revealed a broken tooth. "No mind to that, wife. I voted. In the year 1872 I am a man – a full, free citizen. And I voted!"

Moses told his story – at least most of it – as Lela scurried to gather cloth and cold water to tend her husband's wounds.

"Figured gettin' to the votin' place 'fore crowds got there make it go better in case of trouble," Moses explained. "Felt like the ride in went quick and it didn't take nothin' to find the place." Answering before they could ask, he said, "It was at Mr. Hart's just like we figured."

"What was it like to vote, Papa? How did you do it?" Solomon was full of questions.

"Ain't but Mr. Hart there with three men I never seen to see to the votin'," Moses went on. "Told me just to wait for others first so I moved to the side and waited so's the two men who finally come in made their marks."

"Then you voted, Moses?" Lela asked warily.

"Well, Mr. Hart and me passed the time while I waited and, real quiet-like he let on as to how the men might try to give me some trouble. I said I seen trouble afore so, soon's I could, I went to the table." At this point Moses paused to gather his thoughts and decide just how much of the story he would tell. "Told me I was sure old enough but had to own prop'ty to vote. I show 'em my papers and the deed and the big one whispers to the other, 'Get something for him to read.'"

"Why'd you have to read, Papa?"

"Seems they got special rules." Intent to keep the mood light, Moses explained, "Man got to be twenty-one which ain't too hard to see. Got to own prop'ty and got to read and write. I knowed that was their doin' 'cause them two 'fore me didn't show no deeds or nothin'" Moses took a long drink from the water dipper and continued. "I read the paper they gave me. Must have done that alright because they frowned and said I have to write for 'em."

"What in the world did you write, Moses?" Lela asked curiously.

"Just somethin' that show I knew how I guess. That's another thing them other two didn't have to do, but I wrote down that we come here in 1866 and work hard to build our homestead. Musta wrote good 'nough because they got all fidgety and frownin'."

"But, Moses, none of this explains your face," Lela admonished. "Who hurt you?"

Brushing her question aside with a swipe of his arm, Moses continued. "They knowed they didn't have true reason I couldn't vote 'ceptin they just didn't want me to. He kept his distance but they knew Mr. Hart was there hearin' the whole thing, too. It almost funny how them men squirmed and waited to see Mr. Hart have to leave the store for something. But he didn't."

"Papa?" Solomon asked. "You think he stayed to help you?"

Moses nodded and cut the story short. "Didn't have no true reason to keep me from votin' so I took the paper, went to the counter, and marked by votes. Voted President Grant back in, I did."

"Seemed they got over it all soon's I done the votin' and I got them little things you wrote on the list, said good-byes to Mr. Hart, and headed back this way. Wasn't 'til edge of town seen two of the men. We did our little talkin' and I rode on, so here I am."

Both Lela and Solomon knew there was more to it than that. His appearance wasn't the result of a lively discussion, but if Moses didn't want them to know more, they wouldn't know more. Solomon seethed in silence and his mood turned dark. He was also anxious to get to town and see if Mr. Hart was given a hard time. He now knew that there were those who would punish anyone who stood for right when it suited their purposes.

CHAPTER NINETEEN

1873 -- Fall was slowly approaching. A scorching and waterless summer had worn Solomon down and he was ready for a break. He'd not left the place in over a month except for catching a few fish, a necessity as poorly as the late garden did unquenched in the blazing sun. Even that was hard in the heat. Chores were caught up around the place. Contrasting with the lush spring crops, the meager drought-ridden harvest was in and stored and fire wood stacked ahead of schedule. It was too early for fall planting and their hogs and fledgling cattle grazed lethargically storing what fat they could for winter.

Heading in a generally westerly direction at dawn, Solomon had no idea where he was going or what he hoped to do. He just knew he was glad to be on the trail and Swamp Foot seemed to share his excitement. Tiger was getting lazy and needed to hone his hunting skills. It had been so long he felt only a little guilty about his need to occasionally run away from home. His plan was to have no plan.

At Fayettetown Solomon stopped to water Swamp Foot and refresh himself, quietly tipping his hat and speaking to a couple of people he knew. Remounting, he was off again. The days passed in perfect solitude for rider, horse, and dog. They encountered few people on the trail and none when they left it. An expert woodsman from his earliest childhood, he found enough fish and small game to keep his belly full and enough remainder to share with Tiger. Swamp Foot never had trouble finding grasses, leaves, and even berries to please his palate.

Unsure of how far he had ridden, Solomon knew he was nearing a town when he found a scattering of houses much closer together than usual. He had never been to this tiny but busy little place and needed a few supplies anyway, so he headed to the general store. He noticed was that there seemed to be more dark faces here than he had seen before, although there was a wider mix in Cedar Key including Spanish and even a couple of Orientals. The Freemans and Granny Ma were the only freedmen he knew of in and around New Troy.

Taking that and the shop keeper's behavior as signs of acceptance Solomon tied Swamp Foot under a shade tree and meandered up one side and down the other of the town's single street. This would be a test to see if Tiger could follow his training without being tethered. Feeling comfortable and calm, he returned to the store for a peppermint stick, a treat that always made him think of the goods things of his life. Solomon could tell all the fascinating smells in the place were driving Tiger crazy but the nearly grown pup stayed right at his boy's heel. He would buy some jerky knowing it was more for Tiger than himself. Half of the store was the general merchandise where ladies shopped but on the other side of a three-quarter wall was where ladies never went. Peeking around the wall as he walked around the store Solomon saw that there wasn't much to the dingy saloon. What surprised him was the number of men drinking and bragging at a time when most men should be working.

Standing next to the dividing wall, Solomon heard enough bits of a conversation that he took extra time inspecting the shirts stacked there. He paid for his purchases and stopped to give Tiger praise and a morsel of jerky when they exited the store. He made his way back to the oak tree to wait and watch. "Swampie," he whispered to his faithful horse, "I think you best be ready. We got to be patient but there's somebody here we got to talk to." He appeared to take his ease at the base of the tree as Swampie grazed quietly nearby. "And Tiger," the dog looked up expectantly, "YOU be ready to catch if need be." He was sure Tiger knew exactly what he'd said. "Just hold for now. Hold," he said firmly.

Just about the time Solomon had finished his first peppermint stick and despaired his lack of patience, a large very dark man exited the saloon. It was well into the afternoon and, though it appeared that the man had been there quite a while, he was steady on his feet – even walking with a swagger. "There, boys, see that man there?" Solomon said as he stretched and slowly stood to untie the horse. "Just watch and see what happens."

Cards or a business deal, whatever happened in the saloon seemed to have gone the man's way since he folded a stack of bills and stuffed them into his pocket as he made his way down the street to what passed for a livery stable. The young man wasn't used to lurking around watching people and didn't like the patience and control it required. He might even be wrong about what he heard or that this man was who he thought. But, Solomon watched the rotund man struggle to pull himself onto his burdened old horse and committed himself to finishing his investigation.

The man rode right past Solomon and Swampie as he left town, giving no sign that he even knew they were in the shade of the tree. Once again, Solomon had no plan. He just had to find out who the fat man was. Following at a distance the boy left town after the big man in the dandified hat and suit. Once well out of town their pace increased and they came upon the man as though they just happened to be on the same road together.

Slowing as though to give Swampie a breather, Solomon rode in silence. "Good afternoon, my good man," the man said with a little too much enthusiasm. The boy tipped his hat with a glance at the dog and a grim smile and rode in silence. "Glad to have company on the road. It is such singletary work traveling as I do."

"Oh?" Solomon said leaving space open for the man to answer.

"Indeed yes. It's my lot to travel mile after mile sharing my wares with those who might be helped by them." Assessing Solomon's age and status, the man discounted him as a potential customer but didn't mind the company on the road.

The two rode on, the hefty salesman doing most of the talking with his rambling, regularly inarticulate patter. They dismounted when they reached a small spring to let the horses drink and the man seemed to regain his manners. "So sorry, my boy, I've not even introduced myself," he bellowed. "At your service," he said with a flourish, "my name is Josiah Dukes, the source for working implements of all kinds."

Solomon didn't even hear the last few words as he tried not to flinch or overreact. He fiddled with Swamp Foot's tack as he said, "Dukes, did you say?" He couldn't turn and look at the man.

"Why yes, Josiah Dukes, late of Atlanta but learning my way here in Florida."

"You been this way before?" Solomon asked, hoping his voice didn't betray him. This was the man. Solomon just wanted him to admit what he had done and make payment for it.

"Why yes, it's been a while but I've visionaried some of this territory," Dukes replied. He wiped his round face with a wet handkerchief as he observed, "Though I don't recall it being this hot. I could melt away in this roasting heat."

"Know what you mean," Solomon mumbled thinking Dukes could do with some melting away. "So, that would be couple years ago maybe?"

Unconcerned the man thought a moment. "Sounds about right I suppose. Can't say to a certainness. Met some fine people hereabout, some fine people."

Solomon was sure he'd never heard such a puffed up man before. Resting his hat on the saddle horn he turned to face Dukes. Staring so intensely that the man was forced to look up into his eyes, Solomon had his say. "You stopped by the Freeman place on that trip, Mr. Dukes, and took money for a plow you never delivered." Dukes tugged at his too- tight shirt collar as though he couldn't breathe. "You talked and talked and pretended to be a friend. Worse than that you're one of us – a dark skinned man who should be better." Solmon's hand rested gently on the handle of the whip attached to his side. "Worse still is that you had no intention of delivering on the deal you made."

"Well, er . . .," Dukes sputtered backing toward his horse. "I can explain . . ."

"I'm sure you can," Solomon interrupted. "My name is Solomon Freeman and I believe my father paid you twelve hard-earned dollars he couldn't spare. Add to that the insult and worry you gave my parents I'd say about $50 would serve to cover . . . the interest I believe it's called. It won't make us even but it'll do."

Solomon thought this confrontation would consist of a simple payment so he could forget Josiah Dukes ever existed. He watched and waited while the man fumbled with his pockets. The fat shaking hand reached into his coat and pulled out something shiny. Knife or gun Solomon couldn't tell until it fired just past his head. They were too close for Solomon to do more than lash a short length of the whip out and club Dukes with its hard handle. Before Solomon could strike once, Tiger had Dukes' ankle in a death grip between his teeth. Solomon gave a release command to Tiger, who responded but stood close emitting a low growl. As with the brindle bull Solomon struck quickly from one side then the other until Dukes dropped the light weight pistol and cowered at the young man's feet whimpering.

The boy paused to kick the gun clear and was compelled to pummel the despicable man until he drew blood and the man was a sniveling mass. Predictably, it didn't take long. As though something from behind stayed his hand, Solomon stopped battering Dukes suddenly and looked down in disgust. *Am I more disgusted with myself or Dukes?*

The vile man was hurt and would be scarred but he would soon recover. "Can you hear me, Dukes?" he growled. Without attempting to stand or even look up, Dukes whined affirmatively and Solomon continued as he rifled through the man's coat pockets. "I'm goin' to take fifty dollars from you to make up for the payments you owe my papa and an extra fifty in payment for the lesson I hope you've taken to heart." After taking the money Solomon stuffed the remainder back into a pocket and watched a few bills blow into the nearby scrub.

"Now I'm gon' leave you, but not without giving you something to think on." Dukes rolled to his side and buried his bloody head in his arms. "First, you ain't gon' speak of this to anybody ever. Stay here 'til you healed or go someplace for help, I don't care. But anyone ever speak our names in the same breath I'll haint you like you never seen."

"Now, I recommend you to leave here for good and all. Not just Lafayette County, Dukes, I mean this whole territory. Ain't no room for such scum as you in this world but I reckon it ain't my place to send you from it. 'Bout wish I could. Might make me feel a sight better." Avoiding the temptation to do what he really wanted to do to Dukes, the young man coiled the whip and tied it at his side as he moved toward Dukes' horse. Looking down on the pitiful ball of a man, Solomon went on. "I hear of you anywhere near here or any other place I would ever happen to be you'll be carried out with more than cuts and bruises. That clear?"

The man grunted and nodded his head through his whimpers. Every piercing little whimper made Tiger growl again. Shaking his head with disdain he'd felt for few men, he said, "And for God's sake, man, get yourself a bigger horse to haul your fat ass on." Solomon unsaddled Dukes' poor horse and hefted the saddle onto Swamp Foot planning to drop it in the woods on his way out to inconvenience the evil man a little more. "Come on Tiger, he ain't worth our time." He led Swampie into the woods, taking a last look at Josiah Dukes, and was amazed that a man of such bulk could appear so very, very small.

Somehow Solomon had the ability to remain alert to his surroundings but continue his travels with no particular direction or plan. He could not, however, rid himself of the gnawing anger boiling in him. After several days' travel, he realized he had circled easterly and was approaching Dudley Farm. *Wanderin' brought me here. Guess now is the time.*

He stopped to take the place in. It was a green scarf he saw on this day that gave him immediate relief. He dismounted, watered Swampie, tied the horse to a post, and loosened his cinch. He knew the most likely place to find Mother Mary so he could give her a small gift of brightly printed fabric. They spoke for a few minutes and he wandered toward the edge of the farm speaking to those he knew.

As he approached the little pond, Solomon knew he wasn't alone. He leaned against a tree and gazed across the water – waiting. When Sallie Mae reached around the small tree and gently touched his shoulders he began to shed the tension he had carried for weeks; the restlessness, anger, and confusion were leaving his body as flour flows from a hole it its sack.

Solomon and Sallie Mae spent the afternoon walking through the straw-carpeted piney woods and talking about all that had happened in their lives since they had last visited. Sallie Mae never knew when it would be, but she was confident that Solomon would return to Dudley.

After Solomon walked Sallie Mae to her cabin, he stopped by the back porch of the main house where he found Mrs. Dudley mending. "Mending some, Mrs. Dudley?"

"Land a mercy, I reckon. That man can't go through a single day without rips and tears." Shaking her head and chuckling she added, "You'd think he was just trying to keep me busy as though I have nothing else to do during a day!" Waving a welcome she said, "Come on up, Solomon, and sit a spell."

Mrs. Dudley and Solomon talked for longer than he'd visited with anyone at Dudley except Sallie Mae. He was more than grateful that the woman was warm and understanding. Solomon stood and said, "You have a kind heart, Mrs. Dudley, a real kind heart. I'll see you three months from today then."

The woman smiled up at Solomon and replied, "I'll mark it down, son, and you get on home and get to work!" When he was back on ground level he turned to wave and Mrs. Dudley spoke again. "I'm proud of you Solomon and the way you're carrying out your business."

"Thanks Ma'am. That means a lot to me, it does." He turned and leapt onto Swamp Foot to head home.

The only thing that slowed him at all was the need to bring in some fresh meat so, as he neared home, Solomon paused long enough to bring down a deer and some rabbits. That would be enough to make a different in the stew pot and the smoke house. He arrived home with renewed strength and purpose.

CHAPTER TWENTY

It was a good time to start a new project and three months wasn't long at all. It would be weeks before the new growing season was safely arrived and the project work could be done except on the very coldest days. And really, there weren't so many of those here. Solomon could still make quick trips to Dudley. He'd want to go around Christmas but the time that really mattered was the end of February. *A lot needs to be done before then and I'd better get to it.* The instant his chores were done, he and Tiger could be found circling and measuring the site of their original log cabin. Over time, most of the debris from the fire had been salvaged or cleared away so the area was reasonably smooth. He made notes and cleared and leveled the area all around the original home site.

Moses had tried to be patient and allow his son to share with him what was on his mind. Finally, Moses watched as Solomon wrote in his little notebook and couldn't wait any longer. "Son, you studying on somethin' mighty hard."

Startled, Solomon turned to his father. "Guess I am, Papa, and I'm afraid I need some help."

Solomon thought he saw a rare smile on his father's face and breathed deeply to hear his response. "Guess this is something I've needed to talk about, Papa. Just don't know how you and Mama feel about it."

"Well, son," Moses said, straining his patience, "we can't feel much of nothin' without we know what it is."

"I want to build my own cabin – right here where the first one was. And I want to start it now so it can be done before spring."

Of all the things Solomon might brood about, this was not at all on Moses' list. However, this was obviously important and Moses wanted to do right by his son. "Still a right good spot for a cabin, I'd say. You sure you want to be so close to the bunkhouse?"

"There's some yard between. I hadn't thought it would be a problem. Do you think that's too close, Papa?"

"Reckon not. What you lookin' to build? Somethin' bigger than our little cabin? You got a layout in mind?"

"I think I have enough saved up for lumber so it could be a real house. Nothing grand, but floor and solid and big enough." Solomon began pointing and explaining. "I think adding to the back a ways would be plenty big and raise it up couple of feet off the ground. A fireplace on one end of the front room and cook stove on the other ought to be plenty warm through winter. And I'd sure like to have a water pump right at the sink. Do you think we could do all that, Papa?"

"Good timing, I'd say. You intent on doing this by yourself or you let me and your Mama help?" Moses just had to ask the major question on his mind. "What's bringin' this on, son? You gettin' growed but I didn't know you weren't comfortable in the bunkhouse with us."

Solomon shifted a little and finally looked Moses even in the eyes. "Takin' a wife, Papa, and if I can't give her a house I don't need to be marryin' her."

It was a good thing there was a stump nearby because Moses nearly fell on it when his legs gave way. "A . . . a . . . wife?" The questions just flew out. "Where does she live? How'd you decide this? How come we ain't heard about her? Does your mama know?" Leveling a serious eye on his son, Moses asked, "Why such a hurry, son?"

Solomon laughed a little. "Slow down, Papa. You think maybe we should call Mama out so I can do the tellin' once? Let's move to the shade of the porch and I'll tell you both all about her."

So, the Freemans did just that. They sat on the front porch and Solomon told them all about Sallie Mae. How they met and how she had the ability to calm him and make him confident, how he could talk to her about anything. A little embarrassed about the topic, but he told them right off they needn't worry that it was a rush because Sallie Mae wasn't that kind of girl and he'd not taken any liberties with her.

Lela shook her head with a gentle smile and said, "I knew you were making regular trips to Dudley but never once thought there was a girl. What's she like, Solomon? Are you sure?"

"I'm sure, Mama. Sallie Mae's a hard worker and do most anything – well she's not much for fancy needle work but she can sew a little and I think she'll need to learn some more about cookin' but she's a fine hand with animals and plants and real smart. I been teaching her to read and write some. She never had the chance before but really wants to learn."

"That's fine, son. You know I'll be glad to help, too." "I told her that already, Mama. You'll love her; both of you will love her." With a faraway look on his face he added, "And she's pretty, too. Just tall and slender and real pretty."

"I'm sure she is, son," Moses said, "and you if pick her she'll be welcome here from the start."

Looking like a weight had left his shoulders, Solomon smiled then he laughed. "I'm glad you understand. I wanted you to love her, too."

Acting on her nature, Lela became practical. "So, when is this wedding to happen? At least I know why you've been prowling over the old cabin site. What do you plan?" Before she could throw another out, Moses held up his hand.

"Now that the cat's out of the bag and we know there be lots to talk about, Lela, you best get your list out here. Things slowed considerable so timing's good to just getting things ready for our Sallie Mae." Lela's heart nearly burst with appreciation for Moses' uncharacteristically sweet acceptance of their son's intended. Lela quickly returned with her habitual list and coffee. The three talked and talked while Sarah played quietly.

Within a few weeks there was a large stack of lumber and the foundation and framing on a modest, but much larger than the original cabin, were completed. Knowing to anticipate a rainy spell at this time of year, the next goal was to get the exterior walls up and the roof on the house.

Almost midday the rattle and clatter of a wagon wove through the woods and Lela breathed a prayer of thanksgiving. She refused to say it out loud but Lela was exhausted, feeling as she did when the three of them built the original lean-to. A break would be so welcome especially from the Harkers. Moses and Solomon were equally pleased for a diversion, even a fleeting one.

Only Manuel and Slim accompanied Pete and Elizabeth Harker this trip and both knew their roles. Manuel tended the livestock while Slim helped young Richard down from the wagon. Pete vaulted from Diamond and carefully helped Elizabeth down. As soon as Lela approached her half-sister she stopped dead for a few seconds then squealed, "Betsy! Look at you and how you're glowing!" It was clear that Betsy well into her pregnancy and wouldn't be traveling any more after this trip. At least not for a good while.

With hugs all around, news was shared from both sides and everyone had eaten their portion of a venison stew that Lela had intentionally made to stretch several more meals.

Young Richard approached Solomon shyly. The little boy looked up to Solomon and wanted to shadow him when they were at the Freeman's. It was clear he wanted to ask Solomon something but he was too shy to ask it.

"You get enough to eat, Richard?" Solomon asked lightly.

"Yes, thank you. Miss Lela is a really good cook."

The way the little boy said it Solomon wondered about Miss Betsy, but that didn't matter to anybody except maybe Pete. "Can we go down to the river, Solomon?" the little boy asked. "Pleeease . . ."

Lela noticed Betsy's body going rigid. "Richard, it's much too late in the year to swim," she said in a voice as cold as spring water.

"Oh, no Miss Betsy," Solomon laughed, "I don't mind takin' Richard for a walk and don't have any ideas about going swimmin'!" He could tell Betsy wasn't happy. "He's only six -- probably just needs to run some steam off after the long wagon ride. We won't be long."

Lela added, "They'll be fine, Betsy, Solomon would never let anything happen to Richard."

Betsy sighed and admitted that she knew Solomon was a responsible boy but she didn't relax much. Richard dashed to the wagon and returned with a hat on his head and a little boat in his hand. The two boys, tall and small, turned toward the river and chattered away until they were soon swallowed into the woods.

Pete chuckled, "Look at those two. You'd think they'd known each other forever. It's good for Richard to have an older cousin to look up to." He peaked at Betsy to find that she wasn't convinced that Solomon was her first choice of a role model for her son."

Just about the time Pete and Betsy's things were settled in the bunk house and afternoon chores were done, Betsy and Lela had supper well under way. No matter where on the place Betsy was, Lela saw that her eyes weren't long off the woods where the boys had disappeared. "Betsy," Lela asked, "what are you afraid of? Those boys aren't up to any harm."

"Oh, Lela, I know they mean no harm, but. . .," she paused, struggling to voice her feelings, "Richard's so little and has just started to swim a little. I just worry about everything."

Lela took Betsy's hands in hers and stared at her sister. "We've been together but had different lives. What isn't different is that we are mothers of sons. You can't let Richard know you're fearful of everything he does or wants to do."

Needing her hands free to express herself, Betsy broke away from Lela. "But, what if he's hurt?"

"You do your very best to be sure that hurt isn't permanent," Lela said firmly. "You cannot grow a man if you lay your fears on him. Just think about it, Betsy, and try not to be so quick to show your fears for him." Lela paused to be sure she said the next thing just right. "Betsy, you do know that Solomon would never let anything happen to Richard if there was any way he could prevent it, don't you?"

Betsy stammered just an instant and replied, "Oh, of course he wouldn't. I know Solomon's a good boy." Despite her intent to follow Lela's advice, her face brightened the instant she saw their two sons emerge from the direction of the river. As they came closer, though, alarm returned to her voice. "Richard! What happened? How did your hat get sopping wet? Are you alright?"

Solomon and Richard looked at each other and burst into laughter. "Well what's so funny? There's no reason Richard's brand new hat should be ringing wet!" She tossed her head in exasperation as Lela had seen so many times.

"I'm sorry, Miss Betsy," Solomon explained. The boys stumbled over each other trying to explain their adventure. Richard would put his little boat in the water about ten feet up river from Solomon who would straddle the current on two flat rocks that rose above the low running water. Solomon snagged the boat as it came to him. Burning up his excess energy, Richard ran downriver to get the boat and run back up to put it in again. The current was gentle and fairly straight at that part of the river so it was easy fun.

A breeze came up when Richard bent over to launch the boat and his hat blew right into the water. Solomon laughed and said, "I have to say it was a pretty good trick to get the boat and hop over a couple of rocks and grab the hat before it went right on down to the big Gulf of Mexico!"

"But he did it, Mama, Solomon just jumped from one rock to the other so fast! See? We're alright. It's just my hat that got wet."

Pete stepped in to calm Betsy before she flew too far off the handle. "The boy's fine, Elizabeth. No harm done." He held her at arms' length and waited for her to look straight at him before he spoke further. "Elizabeth, Richard has to be given a chance to be a boy and to grow and become strong. He will be bruised and scraped and possibly even hurt sometimes, but he'll get along fine if you'll just give him a chance."

The big man then knelt in front of six year old Richard and became very serious. "Richard, we want you to grow strong and knowledgeable about the ways of the woods. But your mother worries terribly about your safety. You always must be mindful of how what you do makes her feel."

Nodding his head, and using a new term, Richard said, "Yes, Poppy, I'll be careful and think of Mama. I don't want her to be sad."

Warmed by Richard's name for him, Pete ruffled the boy's hair and reassured the boy. "I know you don't, son. You're a fine boy and we're both proud of you." With a stern look Pete added, "You understand from now on that you are not to go down to the river or spring, or into the woods without someone with you and letting your mother or me know. Are we clear about that?"

"Yessir. Soon I'll be big enough but right now I'm too small to go alone." Pete smiled broadly at his step son's understanding and sent him off to play.

Trying to lighten the tone, Lela laughed, "Oh, I'd hate to remember all the times Solomon's come in with blood someplace – my heart jumping every time." She shook her head. "But look at him now. He can hold his own with about any grown man around. I'm so proud of him for the man he's becoming." Almost as though she had forgotten, she added, "Oh! Speaking of becoming a man, our Solomon's to be married!"

That announcement took over everybody's interest and great discussion ensued about when, where, and what needed to be done. Slim and Manuel were especially excited because they were the only ones there who knew Sallie Mae and could tell the family about her. They gave her high praise and congratulated Solomon. "Just wait 'til Angus hears this!" Slim announced.

The next day Solomon and Slim went to New Troy for building supplies along with a very long list from Lela and Betsy for housewares. They returned with both wagons filled with lumber, nails, and other building materials. In addition, Slim had been given instructions from Pete to purchase two wood cook stoves, an outdoor hand pump, and three indoor hand water pumps. Slim knew this meant hard days to come, mostly for him and Manuel. It would be worth it, though, because of the affection they all held for Solomon and his parents.

CHAPTER TWENTY-ONE

Within a few weeks a host of decisions were made – some of them surprising. Betsy was deemed low risk so the Harkers were to stay through Christmas and until the baby was born. Granny Ma moved into Solomon's bedroom to midwife Betsy and become a permanent part of the family. The sale of her house in town made her secure that she could help the family when needed. The Freeman family was growing and the place was more bustling and exciting than ever before. The face of the homestead changed, too, with important improvements.

Betsy appeared to be more at ease with the homestead and went about making the bunk house a little more like Moses and Lela's side, omitting a cook stove because she would just help Lela with the cooking. With extra strong hands on board, those improvements included an addition to the side of Lela and Moses's living quarters to allow more space and privacy for their growing family.

Granny Ma protested, "Fiddle all these doings. I don't need no special treatment."

"Of course you do, Granny. You've been part of this family for several years now and you deserve everything we can possibly do for you." Lela put her hand on the woman's plump, wrinkled cheek. "Granny, you've been with us for highs and lows. We love you and want you to love being here."

"I already do, Baby, I already do."

With the Harkers taking up the other side of the bunk house, the men needed a place to stay when they were on the homestead. A bunkhouse, smaller than the first, was built a distance from the central living quarters. Once everyone was settled in the men moved on to Solomon and Sallie Mae's cabin and a surprise upgrade for Lela.

It took almost a week to get a pipe drilled down to the underground water source and piped to Lela, Betsy, and Sallie Mae's kitchens but they got it done. All the men took rounds of pounding the pipe into the ground, piece-by-piece through the rocky shelf and into the stream underground. This would be the site of the outdoor pump and watering trough. That was enough to make them all feel their backs and shoulders stiffen and ache but this was to be a complex water system. Trenches were dug from the main well to each house and connected to a smaller pump handle at the sink of each kitchen. Lela was beside herself with this early Christmas gift and hoped Sallie Mae would appreciate hers, too.

As soon as the water system was completed and tested Slim and Pete unwrapped two brand new cook stoves and installed them in the kitchen areas of the two cabins. Solomon and Moses had long before discussed getting water pumped to the house and it was such a big project that Lela couldn't have missed its progress. But the stoves were hidden near the new bunk house and she'd had no idea they were there.

Everyone seemed in on the joke except Lela. Pete and Moses encouraged her to see the progress made in Solomon's house and she was dewy-eyed over the stove. "Oh, how lucky that Sallie Mae is."

Solomon laughed, "Mama, just think. Even if Sallie Mae doesn't cook much with a fine stove like this seems like she'll be near 'bout good as you in no time."

"Oh, Lela," Moses assured her, "don't you worry over this. We'll see to you gettin' one, too. Just they cost pretty dear and Solomon's 'most always had more money than us!" He took her by the arm and said, "Could you come to our house a minute and let Pete and me see if we can rig the pump up just like you want?"

The giggling started almost before Lela was in the front door. One look and Lela's eyes lit like summer stars. She also had a beautiful new cook stove with a sturdy pipe to pull the smoke right away from the house. "Well, no need to stand and look at it. Won't be doing its job without Lela and Miss Betsy get started to cooking," Moses laughed.

Lela clutched her hands and just squealed like a new baby with its first taste of honey water. Betsy went to Lela's side and the women stood arm-in-arm admiring the beautiful new stove.

When she and Betsy served up supper the crowd responded enthusiastically. Lela demurred. "Don't get too over-wrought now, boys," Lela laughed. "I 'spect it'll take some time to learn how to regulate this thing. Might be some burnt here and some raw there, but I'll get the hang of it." She got a little misty-eyed and said, "I don't even know quite who's responsible for it so I thank all of you for this beautiful stove and for the very special little family we are building here."

"Well, Lela, it was sort of a group effort," explained Pete. "But tell us . . . weren't you just the tiniest bit envious to see that Sallie Mae would start out with one and you didn't have one?"

She knew perfectly well that Pete was goading her but she had to be honest. Sheepishly she said, "It's awful but I have to say I was! Oh, I'm so happy that Solomon and Sallie Mae will start out with more than Moses and I had. But I did sort of want one." In the end, there were no complaints from the cooks or the diners and Lela would save many a step and have much more variety in what she could cook and that would be good for everyone. "No more campfire cooking unless I just want to!" Lela proclaimed.

Solomon ambled over to the clothes line where his mother was hanging the wash. It was easy to talk to her any time but especially when her hands were busy.

"But, Mama, you'd love seein' the Dudley place," insisted Solomon.

"I know I will, Solomon, and I'd dearly love to see you and Sallie Mae joined properly." She looked wistfully into the distant woods then shook her thoughts away. "We have to be sensible, though. I can't leave Moses here to handle things even with the others here." She paused trying to find the right words. "Besides, son, you plan to take a few days coming home so you and Sallie Mae can have a little time together."

"I'd figured maybe coming on to our house."

"It's a fine thing you've done, son, making sure Sallie Mae has a house separate from ours. That's important so she can make it a home for the two of you without interference." This was delicate territory and Lela wasn't sure how experienced Solomon was so she was just honest. "A few days alone together without anyone even nearby would be lovely for you both."

"With just the wagon?" he worried.

"Oh, we can be sure you have some food, a lantern, and blankets and an oil cloth in case it rains. The wagon can be quite cozy since there won't be much to carry." They had shifted toward the wood pile and, since he had grown so tall, Lela gestured to Solomon to sit on a stump so she could easily look him into the eye. "Solomon, you know I will be honest with you always. I don't know . . . well, how much you know . . . what your experience . . ."

His face told her all she needed to know. "I can tell you love and respect Sallie Mae and I must assume she feels the same way about you. That's where you start. Getting to know each other in every way possible will take years, especially since you've gotten to know each other by short visits." Lela smiled wistfully and continued. "Your Papa and I are still learning things about each other, and those things change as you go through life. There's no time limit."

"Mama, what if she isn't . . . I don't know . . . I've never . . ."

Lela nodded. "It doesn't matter, son. Try not to be impatient with her or yourself and, little by little, you'll enjoy each other's company more and more. And don't be afraid to talk about these things. When the both of you are comfortable then everything will work out." Solomon appeared relieved when he took his mother's hands in thanks. "You go. Marry Sallie Mae and bring us home a new daughter."

"I will, Mama. You'll like her, I know you will." Lela stood to return to the clothesline. "She's a lot like you." She turned to the boy in puzzlement.

"No," he said, gently waving his hands, "she don't **look** like you, she **is** like you. She's strong and works hard. And she has kind eyes that show me a good heart. That's what I see, Mama." Lela moved to her son and in his gentle embrace her glistening eyes looked Heavenward in thanks that he had found someone so special.

Pulling back to dispel the cloud of sentiment, Lela advised, "Take your time, show Sallie Mae some of your favorite places and tell her about our lives here. And we'll be ready to welcome her home the minute you drive in."

Betsy stood on the porch and looked across the yard for Richard. She and Lela were vigilant about keeping their eyes out for both the children and checked in with each other if they weren't in sight. She didn't see Sarah either, which was odd since the two could spit and fight like cougars but had grown to love each other and spent most of their time together. "Lela?" she called. "Have you see Richard and Sarah?"

Lela came around the end of the house scanning the yard, saying, "Saw them about half hour ago. I thought they were at the chicken yard but I don't see them now.

Suddenly, both women were riveted on Sarah's voice. "Mama, Mama! Aunt Betsy, come quick!" They heard her before they saw her. Hammering stopped at Solomon's house as everyone scrambled toward the little girl's voice. Just as they sighted her, they saw Solomon running as fast as he could while carrying Richard in his arms.

Pete immediately went to Betsy as she screamed, "Richard . . . noooo!" Pete stilled her so she wouldn't run and hazard the baby. His heart pounded nearly out of his chest but Pete knew he had to keep a calm head.

Solomon was laboring and Slim was larger and stronger so the big man rushed to take Richard gently from Solomon's arms. Lela had grabbed a quilt and spread it on the ground in the shade. "Here, Slim, put him here." As Richard lay on the quilt, Solomon flopped down on his knees trying to tell what happened between gasps.

Betsy heard an echo of herself scream, "I knew you couldn't be trusted, you careless, sorry ni..." Pete clapped his hand over her mouth before the words could come out and knew she was in trouble. She fainted into his arms.

Just as Pete turned he saw Granny Ma on the porch. "Here, Pete, come on and let's put her in her bed." Pete looked forlornly at Richard and Granny commanded,

"Come on now, Pete. Ain't nothing but a shock but she too close to time for many of those. Lela'll do what can be done for Richard."

"I know, Granny," Pete mumbled, moving toward their front door. "I need to be with Richard, too."

He was sopping wet and cold so they knew he'd been in the river. Lela immediately turned Richard on his side to press any water from his body that she could. "Do you know what happened, son?" she asked Solomon.

"We told him, Mama, we all told him not to go to the river."

"We know son, but he couldn't resist the adventure I reckon," said Moses. "Thing now is to tell us what happened so your mama know the best thing to do for him."

"Thank God for Sarah. She saw Richard go into the woods on that side and first went to catch up with him."

"I 'membered we weren't 'posed to go by ourselves, Papa. I came back," the frightened little girl explained. Richard looked so small and weak even to her.

"Sarah ran back and found me and we went toward Richard. His little boat was in the river caught up in a snag near the rocks I used the other day." Solomon gasped again. "Looks like the boat got caught and he thought he could hop the rocks like he saw me do. Me and Sarah didn't see it happen but he must have slipped on a rock and hit his head. There wasn't much blood that I saw, just a bump. He was just floatin' in a little pool between rocks."

As her hands massaged and prodded, Lela said, "He's wet and too cold. Moses, get blankets from the house and men, move him over by the campfire for now and build it up some." She continued examining the little boy's eyes and limbs through his involuntary shivering. "Nothing is broken and he does have a goose egg on his head already. He's breathing better but it's still weak."

Pete approached the group and knelt next to Lela, reaching toward Richard. "I think he'll be alright, Pete. It's his head that worries me." When she glanced at Pete's face, Lela knew he was ripped down the middle. She knew he loved Betsy and had grown to think of Richard as his own, even to the point of legally changing his name.

"How's Betsy?" Lela continued to bathe Richard's head and check his eyes.

"I think she's alright. Granny wanted to examine her and when she comes to I want to be able to tell her about Richard. He was so limp, I think she thought he was dead." Pete's hand stilled Lela's and he looked from her to Moses. "I'm sorry for what Elizabeth almost said. I don't think she really feels that way; it just bubbled up from emotion."

"We know that," Moses answered for them. "Miss Betsy come a long, long way in her thinkin' since we left Hill's Run. All our lives changed and maybe hers more than anybody's. I been a little surprised she seems to like it here where it not so fancy."

Lela defended Betsy, too. "It takes a long time and a lot of effort to change our deep feelings about important things. Betsy's made lots of changes in her thinking but life- learned lessons are hard to shake sometimes. We'll all keep working at living in the here and now."

"She's not quite far enough along to deliver early, Lela, and I couldn't stand losing another child." Pete's voice cracked as he thought of his young son years before and the man he might have become. He knew that was what had attracted him to Solomon when they first met.

"Oh, Pete, Granny's a good midwife and Betsy's still plenty young and healthy enough. Let's not buy trouble before we have to. We must keep our faith and help her keep hers."

Granny Ma waddled slowly across the yard to get a cup of coffee at the fire. Pete was clearly alarmed that Betsy had been left alone. Or worse yet, that she had lost the baby or died herself. "Don't get unscrambled Mr. Pete. Betsy restin' well. I just wanted a cup of coffee and move my bones a little."

"How is she, Granny?" asked Lela. "And the baby?" "Oh, she a strong girl, Lela. I think she and the baby be fine. It were a shock, though, to her and me, too, seeing that poor little boy hangin' so limp."

Just then came a low moan from the injured boy. Everyone reached for the child. Lela spoke. "Richard? Richard?" she said softly. "How do you feel, Baby?"

"Mama?" he whispered weakly. "I have hurt on my head."

Just as he had when Solomon had a head injury, Pete moved in and comforted his step-son. "It'll be fine, son. You just rest for now and you'll feel fine." Pete looked at Lela and pointed at his own eyes with his pointer and third fingers. Lela nodded and they knew they would have a long few days ahead. "Richard," Pete explained, "I'm going to pick you up very carefully and take you to Solomon's bedroom but I don't want you to move around – especially your head." The boy nodded.

Soon Richard was comfortably propped up in Solomon's bed with Solomon at his side keeping him occupied with stories and practicing counting and the alphabet. Anything to be sure he didn't fall asleep and fail to regain consciousness.

Pete and Lela paused on the porch between their front doors. "You're wise to put him in Solomon's room, Pete. And he'll love spending more time with Solomon." Pete's forehead was all scrunched up. "And if there was a problem with Betsy," Lela reassured him, "Granny would have come to get us."

"I hope you're right, Lela. I just don't think I could stand losing a second family." Pete paused in contemplation, "For all her little high and mighty ways, Betsy's really a good woman and I love her Lela."

"Oh, Pete, I know that. That's why I don't pay so much mind when she starts telling me what to do."

"I know but I can't help worrying. If I can give her a good report on Richard she'll be greatly relieved and I wanted to avoid Richard hearing something if Betsy was in pain or . . . anything."

Lela's hand on his arm was the physical signal of her support. "I know, Pete. I just think it's all going to work out. I had thought, though, in preparation for the baby maybe Richard could stay in Granny's room since it's a little farther away and doesn't share a wall."

"Do you think she would mind?" Lela's look answered him. "Oh, of course she wouldn't mind. Besides, she'll be with Betsy and so will you. I'm so thankful for that, Lela." Turning toward his door Pete stopped suddenly and whirled around. "Lela! I have to speak with Sarah and thank her for being so brave and doing the right thing. Without her I hate to think what would have happened to Richard."

"That would be a lovely thing to do, Pete. It would make her feel very grown up and I think she looks forward to not being the youngest any more. But after you see to Betsy. Now shoo!"

Lela leaned against the wall and shook her head. *Well, Betsy's going to need to rest and be sure her fright didn't hurt that baby and young Richard will need to stay awake and occupied a day or two before he can rest. That just beats all.*

CHAPTER TWENTY-TWO

Within a few days Betsy was up and able to resume some of her chores, feeling much better for being useful again. Richard still had occasional headaches and he would have a little scar on the side of his forehead, quite a source of pride, but otherwise seemed to be fine, as well. He rejoined Sarah tending to the chickens and piglets and whatever else Lela and Betsy found that young hands could do. That was just life – as soon as hands were able to do a task they needed to get busy doing it.

Pete had has his talk with both Sarah and Solomon with Solomon crediting Sarah for alerting him. Sarah had been traumatized by the sight of Richard so frail and lifeless but once he was back in sync with her she was better. Pete also assured the Freeman children that Richard would be doing no more little explorations without proper permission and company. He had come out of his original shyness and had quite a streak of boyish daring, but his river adventure was enough to frighten him into being more careful and, hopefully, more obedient – at least for the time being.

In fact, Richard and Sarah were diligent about cautioning each other and keeping each other on the right side of the rules. When she brought cool water to the men as they worked to finish Solomon and Sallie Mae's house, Lela told Solomon, "I swear, those two are just like a little old married couple the way they direct and protect each other."

Solomon laughed. "Isn't it good for them to have each other, though? Sort of like sisters need to spend time together?" Lela smiled in agreement and took water to the rest of the men.

Moses and Lela were enjoying a very early cup of coffee at the communal cook fire they still enjoyed just for coffee and Moses seemed even more quiet than usual. Lela knew she might not get much of an answer but she had to ask, "Moses, what are you thinking on so seriously?"

Another swig of coffee seemed to give words to his thoughts. "Just thinkin' about our boy, Lela. Things happ'nin' so fast I can't hardly keep up. All the changes here and more people. Guess I'm just caught in the storm of it all."

"I know what you mean," Lela sighed. "Our boy getting married and I know we'll like her but it's just so sudden."

"To us maybe, but must not be so sudden for him!"

"Are you sure you're comfortable with the expansions and Granny Ma?"

"Place sure is lookin' different but Granny Ma 'bout the only grandparent our children have and she loves them so much." After a pause, he continued. "Surprised that Betsy seems alright with all this. Does she say much to you? She's being good help, ain't she?"

"I was worried about her, too. But, Moses, she seems fine – maybe having close company and useful things to do is good for her. I was afraid she would be . . . I don't know, a loner? Even expecting service, especially with the baby coming."

Moses nodded, noticing Pete and Betsy making their way to the fire, so he reflected. "Well things surely different from when we first came here. Just look how far we come, Lela. Our boy gonna start out in a house – not a cabin but a house proper." Lela leaned in to Moses and he put his arm around her shoulders. "Our boy doing good and I'm right proud of him." Lela's heart sang and she hoped Moses would find a time to say those words Solomon soon.

The approach to Christmas was full of excitement and flurries of work. Pete and Manuel had made a trip to Madison to get supplies of all kinds. They needed food staples, some clothes for Betsy and the new baby, and house warming and Christmas gifts. Richard and Sarah having a wonderful Christmas, getting the baby born safely, and having a special place for Solomon to bring Sallie Mae were the priorities immediately after the many daily chores required on the farm.

The little community that had emerged on the Freeman homestead developed a steady, happy rhythm. Each person's talents and abilities tended to the daily chores and the new projects. Almost everyone had gathered up their coins and made a quick trip to either New Town or Fayettetown to buy gifts or materials for gifts. Christmas secrets were in the wind and special efforts were made to look to each other's needs. Lela wished every season was met with such cheer and good intentions.

There was no way to mask the water system but Lela was so thrilled with the thought of finally cooking inside – and on a fine wood stove instead of the fireplace – Christmas for her had been perfect already. Now she, Betsy, and Granny were working hard to get all of the preparations done for the biggest, grandest Freeman Christmas celebration ever.

It had become such a central part of the place, the entire population of the Freeman Farm gravitated to the camp fire early on Christmas morning. Lela and Granny had biscuits and sausage gravy warming to serve and the men saw to all the morning chores so they wouldn't miss anything about the holiday.

Betsy brought Richard and Sarah, rubbing their sleepy eyes, still in their night clothes and bundled in blankets. Once all were gathered, Pete opened his Bible to Luke and read the story of Jesus' birth and Manuel began played a soft and haunting song on his guitar. When he began to sing in Spanish, which only Solomon could follow, they all knew that this was a rare and reverent moment that captured what they believed and trusted.

When the music ended, Moses stood holding this hat to his heart and offered a blessing. "Lord, you blessed us with Jesus and you blessed us with each other and you blessed us with what this place is turnin' into. We hope we always try to measure up to what you give us and do with it what you want. Thank you for our life in freedom. Amen." And there were "amens" all around the fire.

The tone changed quickly as the families dug into breakfast and bundles large and small seemed to come from nowhere to find themselves in hands all around. Most were homemade with great care and special thoughts of the person to receive it. From silly to sentimental, "thank yous" rang through the woods. Naturally, great focus was on Richard and Sarah as they found socks filled with nuts, oranges, and peppermint sticks. These were rarities and the children were both thrilled with such treats.

Pete presented Richard with his very first knife, a small pen knife with only one blade, and a caution that there would be some lessons in its use before he would be allowed to carry it regularly. Sarah was speechless over the new dress Lela and Betsy made for the fine doll Solomon had given her from his last trip to Way Key. She had become rather prissy for a farm girl and loved such finery. Betsy explained that it was the kind of ball gown a young lady would wear to her first big party. "Maybe I can have one someday!" the little girl exclaimed. Both children were excited about new clothes and were ready to play with their hand carved wooden toys. Both were reading well and each got a brand new book of their own calling out to their mothers that these must be the night's story time subject.

There were mostly practical gifts such as clothes and tools. When Richard and Sarah opened their final boxes they found identical black, wide-brimmed Stetson hats. They were both delighted to look across the fire where their hero was putting on his own identical new hat. "Looky here, Boss," Slim said to Pete and the company, "we got us three matchin' cow hunters now!" The hands relished their places in the family, as well, the useful but appreciated items like new belts, spurs, and shirts they were given.

The group sat and visited, gave thanks, and reminisced as breakfast was cleaned away then drifted to put away or try out their Christmas gifts. These were not people accustomed lavish holidays and, to many, Christmas at the Freemans' wouldn't have been considered extravagant. But it was far more than most of them had experienced and they were appreciative of such generosity from their friends and family. Manuel settled in comfortably near the fire and played and sang for over an hour, voices joining him when tunes were familiar. Moses and Pete stood at a distance watching the mostly quiet bustling with pride and satisfaction at the lives they were building.

CHAPTER TWENTY-THREE

On a working farm, there wasn't much time to linger in the holiday glow although spirits did seem to stay cheerful longer than usual. The day after Christmas the Freeman Farm was back to normal with regular animal and garden chores and finishing the construction of Solomon's house. The extra hands would remain there at least until after Betsy and Pete's baby was born and they could travel to Madison. Slim and Manuel tackled clearing another field for production and Pete and Moses enlarged Lela's kitchen garden, making sure it was large enough and fenced strongly enough to feed them through the seasons and keep critters out. The chicken house and pen were also rebuilt and enlarged much to Sarah's delight since the chickens were her primary responsibility.

The new year brought some cold days limiting chores to the basics necessary for the survival of people and animals. Luckily, however, it was a mild winter overall. Granny was certain that she was doing very well with her pregnancy but, understandably, Betsy tired easily as she neared her term so she spent much of her time teaching Richard and Sarah lessons, reading them stories, mending and other hand work. One night as Lela and Moses were retiring Lela made an observation. "Moses, I can't believe the difference in our place. Just having extra hard working hands made such a difference. How will we ever thank Pete, Slim, and Manuel?" Another thought, almost a fear, occurred to Lela. "How will we get along without those extra hands, Moses, with all the expansion?"

"Know what you mean, Lela. We at such a head start on planting in the spring ought to make us a good year forsure." Moses paused then added, "You reckon they've liked bein' here as a big family?"

Lela laughed lightly. "If you'd told me Betsy would be so content and glad to join in the work I'd have thought you'd gone daft for certain. But, Moses, she really is more settled and . . . well, just different than I've ever seen her."

"We ain't seen her as grown lady so hard to say but I seen the same thing." Not knowing quite how to proceed Moses just came right out with it. "You reckon they be happy stayin' here permanent?" Lela gasped. "Pete got his bank business in Madison but don't have to live there all the time I don't reckon."

"It's certainly something to think about. Betsy has even been able to give Richard some space and time for himself."

"I was worried for that little boy a while there, even with Pete as his daddy."

"Do you know what it is, Moses? Do you know? It's really not so complicated."

"What are you talkin' about, woman?"

"I'm talking about Betsy and Pete having each other, and that little boy, and soon another baby. It doesn't matter to Pete that Richard's not his blood. He's even going to adopt him so his name can be Harker. Betsy and Pete both finally have something they've needed and searched for since that awful war was well started."

"Is it that easy, Lela? It means that much?"

"It means that much to me, Moses. What kind of life and contentment could I have without you and Solomon and Sarah?"

Moses took his wife into his arms and knew she was right because they shared the same kind of need for each other and family that Pete and Betsy did.

The men scattered to fill a long list of items needed from town and work on projects they saw to be done. There was even a little more dawdling around the fire or on the front porch of the big bunk house after supper with things less pressing.

His house finished but for some of the things Lela, Betsy, and Granny planned to do, Solomon took a couple of days for a wander. Slim and Manuel continued rough breaking the new field so it would be ready for planting and Pete returned to Madison for a few days to handle business there. Moses spent a good part of each day taking a mule into the woods to drag logs in to saw and split for firewood. Especially with two wood stoves and the camp fire to feed, keeping up with the wood supply would be harder than ever.

Moses felt weak as he brought the mule in from the field. He couldn't hold out to tend the mule -- just dropped the reins and turned toward the house. This massive man, once a tower of strength, leaned against a tree. His face was pocked and distorted from gun powder burns, shoulders slumped and tilted left favoring the old wound, and weak with fever and utter defeat. He took a step toward the house and fainted soundlessly.

When Lela rounded the corner of the house the laundry basket tumbled to the ground scattering clean clothes like their shattering lives. "Noooooooo!" she screamed as she raced to her husband's body. There was no way to know how long he had been unconscious.

He wasn't dead but his pulse was weak and his body was on fire. He had lost weight in recent months but she still wasn't strong enough to get him into the house. "Oh, Lord God, please give me the strength," she prayed as she strained. The best she could do was roll him over, cushion his head, cover him tightly with blankets, wipe his brow, and drip cool water on his lips hoping he would come to and quench his thirst.

Sarah, old enough now to know something was wrong, helped Lela bathe her daddy's face with cool cloths. Richard sat nearby ready to run for more cold water. Lela's scream roused both Betsy and Granny Ma who came to her as quickly as they could. All the men were gone so they tended Moses there on the ground, trying to make him as comfortable as possible. Betsy and the children stayed with Moses while Lela and Granny Ma rushed to their herbal collection to discuss Moses' symptoms and brew medicinal teas.

A couple of hours later, Slim and Manuel came in from the field and raced to Moses who was now sitting up against the tree. "Oh I be alright, Lela. Don't fuss over me," Moses said hoarsely.

"Let us get him in to his bed, Lela," offered Slim. "Then you can tend him better and maybe you and Granny can figure out what's the matter with him."

Moses pushed Slim's hands back grousing, "Get your hands off me. I can get up." But the big man couldn't get up by himself. He couldn't control his limbs and his voice sounded strange. Trying to give him the needed support and let Moses feel he was doing most of the work, they finally got him settled in his bed and undressed so Lela could tend him better. Once Moses was settled Slim and Manuel rushed outside to feed and stable the animals and finish other chores before dark. They assured Lela that all she needed to do was call and they would do whatever needed doing. Otherwise, they'd stay close by but out of the way.

"Thank goodness we have the inside pump now," Lela whispered as she brought in fresh cooling cloths. "We need to use towels to cover his whole body, it's so hot. Keep rotating them so he can get cooled down. This fever is alarming."

Within five hours, Moses was sitting up; his complexion mostly cleared and coloring normalized. He'd taken a little sassafras tea every ten minutes and the fever had broken. He was feeding himself soup and complaining that they were making way too much fuss over him. Granny Ma sat with Moses and guided Lela in her treatments. Betsy was at a point that she needed to rest when possible so she made sure there was a hearty stew on the stove for anyone who got hungry. There wouldn't be a scheduled evening meal on this night. She made sure Richard and Sarah had supper and settled them in the living area with books and a puzzle. They were good helpers, too, keeping cool water in the bowl for Moses and getting messages to Slim and Manuel. How very thankful Lela was for those two men. They had become just as much uncles to Solomon and Sarah as Pete was.

Betsy had developed confidence in Granny and Lela's medical knowledge but she still wished that Pete was there. She wasn't due for another few weeks and he probably couldn't do a thing for Moses that wasn't already being done but she yearned for his presence all the same. She and the children moved into the Harker side sleeping well. They were fresh enough and Moses was improved enough to send Lela and Granny to Granny's rooms for much needed rest.

It took a full week for Moses to return to a full day's work and even then he took rests – only because Lela monitored him and forced him to. He had to admit to her that he could feel the difference since his illness though. He wasn't too stubborn about resting throughout the day.

Solomon returned laden with game to dress and hang in the smoke house and Moses wasn't in crisis any more so he waited to talk with Lela about his father.

"Mama, what happened to him?" Solomon asked when they finally found time to speak privately.

"I don't know, son, I just can't be sure." Lela was still exhausted because, as Granny said, "She think she the onliest one can do for him." As she filled her son in on the details of the week she said in frustration, "Heart? Something eating at his insides?" She looked blankly at her son. "Maybe this place just killed him. Just slowly, wickedly sucked the life right out of him."

"No, Mama. He's not dead yet and from the look of it he's coming back pretty well." Looking across the yard at his father he added, "It's sure something happened though that might not ever be completely fixed."

Pete had returned from Madison, much to Betsy's delight and relief and he brought big news. He and Betsy had discussed the possibility and Pete announced that they had bought one hundred acres adjoining the Freeman Farm so they could be true neighbors and partners. That brought cheers of celebration all around and things were almost got back to normal at the Freeman Farm. Granny and Lela were on careful watch for any signs that Betsy was in labor, the men continued to do everything possible to be ready for spring planting when the weather broke warm and the almanac said what should be planted when.

In some ways time was flying and in other ways Solomon thought the clock wasn't moving at all. It was almost time for Solomon to go to Dudley for Sallie Mae and he worked feverishly to put some special touches on the house. And he was nervous.

It was the day before he was to leave for Dudley and Solomon was helping Moses mend the hog pen and corral. "Son you jumpy as a toad frog." Moses straightened to look at his son. "Somethin' you want to talk 'bout, son?"

"I don't know, Papa. I don't even know what's in my head." Following Moses' lead, Solomon moved toward the river where they usually cooled down during a hot day's work. Moses knew already, but waited for Solomon to find his words.

"Papa, I been thinkin' about Sallie Mae all the time."

"I know that, son," Moses quietly teased. "You've found most any little excuse to buy or sell at Dudley that you could just as well have done in New Town. Can't hide feelin's like you got for that little girl, son. They just don't cover up." Solomon dipped his head. "No, boy, don't you be 'shamed of that. If I didn't see them feelin's in you I'd be worried."

"I know she's special, Papa. I know that surely. I just don't know . . . the drive back . . . bringing her here permanent . . ."

In a rare fatherly gesture, Moses put a hand on Solomon's shoulder and looked him eye-to-eye. "Son, this gal's your pick. I reckon she's picked you, too, or you wouldn't be going to get her. Clear to see your feelin's be right. Two of you will go through the good and the bad, the easy and the hard and you hang tight to one another you do just fine in this world. I know you been talkin' to your mama 'bout this and I know she told you the right of it. All I can tell you is you see to your Sallie Mae. You used to being a lone wolf and you got to consider her thoughts and feelin's." Solomon nodded. "You two matched with each other proper, it'll work out. You just be slow and get to know one another better. I know your gal's a hard worker but she's a woman, too. Don't you forget bein' tender. Little nice things mean lots to a woman."

Solomon hung his head. "Papa, I never. I have strong feelin's for Sallie Mae, but I never even near . . ."

"I know, son. I be surprised if you had. Don't figure Sallie Mae that kind a gal." Knowing Solomon still wasn't sure, he added, "Hard as it is to believe it a natural thing and you figure it all out in time. Slow and steady, son, all this will work out right."

"That's a lot of what Mama said, Papa," the boy said almost shocked that his parents were both so wise. "We won't take too long; I know you'll need us back here."

"You're not to worry about that, not even when you're settled into your house. One thing your mama and me didn't have in that first year was chances to slip away from work sometimes. You a hard worker but you can take a few hours or a day here and there to do something just the two of you together and your mama and me can carry the place just fine. And Sarah's getting to be good help now, too. 'Sides, we got way more help on the place now than ever."

Moses laughed quietly, "'Course by time you get back here there prob'ly be another little person on Freeman Farm and Sarah thinks she gonna be in charge of the new baby!"

"You're probably right about that, Papa. Sarah likes to take charge. I hope Betsy will find little things Sarah can help her with."

Ironically, Sarah raced up to her big brother with a big hug as soon as her papa turned to walk away. Solomon knelt on a knee and held his pretty little sister for a minute saying, "Hey, what's this all about?"

"I know you're going to bring Sallie Mae back and I saved this from my Christmas sock for you to give to her." She pulled a peppermint stick from her pocket and held it out to Solomon.

"Well, I say Miss Sarah Freeman, that's a very nice thing you've done and Sallie Mae will feel very special to have it." His voice lowered and he looked seriously into his sister's eyes. "You know things will be sort of different when we come back."

"I know." She didn't sound happy. "Mama said you and Sallie Mae would live in your new house and have your own home. It sounded like you wouldn't be part of us anymore."

"No, no, Sweetpea. Thing will be different and I won't be in the house with you and Mama and Papa but I'll still be working and doing chores and all the same. Just think, when Sallie Mae gets here you'll have a brother AND a sister. Did you think of that?"

"Will she like me, Solomon?"

"Of course she will. How could she not like you? But we do need to be patient and helpful because all of this will be new to her. You know every farm does things different and we'll need to help her learn about Freeman Farm. Can you help her sweetly and patiently?"

"I'll try." She thought a moment to be sure she had asked everything she wanted to. "Mama said I wasn't to just go into your house. She said I was to knock and be invited in – just like strangers do."

Solomon laughed, "I wouldn't say like strangers, baby girl, but it would be nice to knock. Just like you do on the Harker's door. It's just good manners to knock first at a family's house. And that's what Sallie Mae and I will be – a new family." Noting the shock in her eyes, he quickly added, "Oh, no! We'll always be family altogether but Sallie Mae and I will have our own household. We won't always eat all together like we have before but you won't even miss me 'cause I'll still be right here on the place."

He gave her another tight hug, sent her on her way, and hoped Sallie Mae would like his family. He couldn't seeany reason not to love them, but maybe they would be too different from what she's used to. *I can't think on that now. We'll just make it work.*

Very early the next morning everyone was nervous for Solomon and excited about this next step in his life. Moses caught him checking the wagon to be sure all was safely stowed and tied down. "Your Mama and me was talkin' last night and I found a piece in the Bible that said, "I go the way of all the earth; be strong, therefore, and prove yourself a man." Solomon knew that if his father was quoting scripture he was very serious. "That's what you doing today, son. What you been doin' a right good job of. You provin' yourself a man. Just remember it ain't the big, hard things a man does that talk loudest. It's being honest and true and hard workin' and mindful of others."

"Thank you, Papa. I'm not sure I've ever really told you, but I do thank you for everything," Solomon said through a constricting throat. "You've taught me to be a good man."

Moses offered his hand to Solomon in a way different from ever before. He acknowledged his boy as a man. Solomon rubbed Tiger where he was tied to a tree, smiled at his mother, waved at the others, and mounted the wagon to fetch his bride.

[1] I Kings 2:2

CHAPTER TWENTY-FOUR

It took Solomon several hours to make his way to Dudley Farm. This gave him far too much time alone to ruminate over what he was about to do. He never doubted that it was right; he just hoped he could make Sallie Mae happy and provide well for her and the family he assumed they would have. At one moment he felt confident and very grown up and the next like a little boy embarking on a mysterious adventure. He wasn't sure what Mrs. Dudley had planned but knew there would be a little ceremony and some refreshments. She had said, "Just show up in your best duds and Mother Mary and I will take care of the rest."

Solomon showed up. He didn't see Sallie Mae anywhere which bothered him. He'd never been to a wedding of any kind so he didn't know what to expect. Mrs. Dudley took him in hand reviewing what was planned and introducing him to the circuit riding preacher. He was sure his parents hadn't had the blessing of a real preacher but thought they would be pleased that he and Sallie Mae would. They would be the first of anyone in his world to do more than jump the broom.

When Mrs. Dudley told him to stay with the preacher and he heard music on a fiddle, Solomon's stomach flipped and churned worse than ever – even worse than having to haggle business with Captain Dudley. Mrs. Dudley had thrust a bunch of camellias wrapped in ribbon and whispered that he was to present them to Sallie Mae when she walked to his side. His hands were so cinched he hoped he didn't break all the stems.

Then, the little crowd parted and Sallie Mae walked toward him. Solomon couldn't breathe. She looked like an angel in a soft pink dress and a halo of tiny flowers. Once they made eye contact all the flutters in Solomon's stomach disappeared. He found himself standing taller and he didn't want to blink for fear of losing sight of her. When she neared him he stepped forward to hand her the flowers. He held her hands for an instant under the flowers and between them the bouquet vibrated nervously. He was ready for the rest of his life.

Knowing he would have to tell the women at home every single detail, Solomon tried to focus on what was happening. It was hard, though. All he could do was gaze at Sallie Mae. It was pretty clear that this preacher hadn't overseen a wedding of slaves or former slaves; he probably didn't want to either. He was also pretty sure Mrs. Dudley had made sure that the preacher got everything legal and blessed properly. They prayed and repeated vows and Solomon had a wide gold band with delicate lacy etching all around it that slipped easily onto Sallie Mae's finger.

The young groom knew at first chance Sallie Mae would take the circlet from her finger and study it carefully. He would tell her how he bought it from a Cuban ship's captain and he had the watchmaker in Cedar Key put the word inside the circle. Four little letters – *amor*. Before he knew it the preacher cleared his throat and said, "You may kiss your bride." Solomon took Sallie Mae's hands and kissed her lightly and her smile lit the day. They turned to face the crowd as a married couple but the ceremony couldn't be completed until they looked at each other, grinned, and jumped in one motion over the broom lain on the ground. Cheers rose from the guests.

What happened next must surely have been a first for Dudley Farm – there were cakes and cookies along with punch and punch with extra. It wasn't so much that everyone mixed and mingled together but that the Dudley family andmost of its workers – light and dark – were there. Maybe it was Mrs. Dudley's affection for Solomon or the company's respect for Mother Mary. Maybe it was because Sallie Mae, being orphaned at birth, had literally been raised by the entire group. It was a sight to behold and one he hoped he could describe to his parents for it had been their hope that what they had at Freeman Farm would be possible far beyond its boundaries.

Before long Captain and Mrs. Dudley took their places on the back porch and the group quieted. Mrs. Dudley waved the bridal couple to join them. *Oh, Lordy, please don't let them ask me to talk.* Solomon relaxed a little when their hostess made a little speech. "The Captain and I thank you for being here today. We wanted to make it a little special for our young couple and I think maybe we did." Applause scattered through the group then she continued. "I'm not sure we can describe what Sallie Mae means to us – ALL of us. We've all taken part in her raising and I'm thinking maybe we did pretty well at it." This time it was laughter that interrupted her. Turning to Sallie Mae and Solomon she concluded. "Sallie Mae, I can't imagine what this place will be without you but we can't keep our little birds in the nest forever. Solomon, you are to bring her with you when you come this way on business now. We can't go so long without seeing her."

Solomon nodded solemnly and said softly, "Yes, ma'am."

The groom almost shuddered when he realized the Captain was to say something, too. "I'll say I wasn't high on this young stripling when I first saw him. Few years of havin' to do business with him just about convinced me he might be alright. Looking hard at Solomon, he added, "That don't mean I won't still bargain hard, boy." Even Solomon laughed. "For those of you who don't know how serious he's takin' this, Solomon has built Sallie Mae a house to start their lives together." Surprise and approval rippled through the crowd. "Sallie Mae, you've chosen well and Solomon, you hurt this little girl the whole of Dudley Farm will come down on you, you hear?"

Again, a solemn nod and, "Yes, sir."

"Gettin' late enough now, you two should be on your way. Don't worry over it until you are settled at home you'll find a few little things from me and Mrs. Dudley and from all of the people here. We'll be wishing you safe journey to your new home and new life together." As Mrs. Dudley hugged Sallie Mae the Captain shook Solomon's hand. The couple joined hands and made their way to the wagon that had been decorated with greenery and what flowers were available in the cold season.

All was laughter and cheer as they drove toward their home until Solomon noticed Sallie Mae turning to send a kiss to the tiny old woman standing in front of the rest of the group seeing them off. Solomon reached for her hand and said, "You'll miss Mother Mary most of all won't you? Don't worry. It's not that far and we'll have plenty of reasons to come this way." Sallie Mae leaned toward him a little and put her head on his shoulder reassured and happy with her new role as Mrs. Freeman.

They drove only about an hour when Solomon pulled into the forest and stopped the wagon. "Oh, Solomon," Sallie Mae said, "you planned to stop here all along. Look what you've done." He helped her down from the wagon and spun her around so he could see her dress again. "I've never had such a dress before but it's not terrible practical. Not so warm neither!"

He grabbed a blanket from the wagon and wrapped her in it, leading her to the log that sat in front of a fire pit all ready to be lit. "You just sit right there ma'am, and I'll get this little fire going and warm up something for us to eat."

Solomon joined his bride on the log and looked straight forward. Sallie Mae realized that he had set their first camp together facing west so they could see the beautiful fireball sun set through the giant pines, the rays grandly coloring the sky. They just sat for the longest time watching the sunset together. When they only had the firelight Solomon offered Sallie Mae a bite of smoked ham. "I'll do my best to give you a life as perfect as the sunset, Sallie Mae."

She offered him a bite and said, "Today was the perfect start to that life, Solomon Freeman."

They ate and talked late into the night and rested blissfully in the cocoon of soft quilts Lela and Moses had prepared for them in the wagon. For the next four days, dressed far more sensibly and comfortably, they wove their way through the woods and rivers stopping whenever they pleased. Solomon showed her some of his favorite spots along the way and told her all about the adventures he had at each as he traveled back and forth from home to Dudley. She hadn't been beyond Dudley and was as wide-eyed and as Solomon had been on his first cow hunt with Pete Harker.

CHAPTER TWENTY-FIVE

By the time Solomon and Sallie Mae neared the farm, they were comfortable with each other and ready to embark on their lives together. Solomon was proud that he would soon be introducing her to his parents and the extended family of Freeman Farm. He knew she would fit in well and add to the success of the farm in important ways. He also knew that his parents would welcome and love her just because he did. She would immediately be family.

Sallie Mae, as secure as she was with Solomon and as peaceful and wondrous as the past few days had been, was as skittery as a new calf. Still amazed that they would live in a brand new house built just for her, she hoped Solomon's family would like her and that she would be able to learn what she should to carry her weight on the farm. They could all read and do figures and, for the first time in her life, the new wife felt somehow different or less. Solomon didn't see her that way, but her lack of book learning was her biggest insecurity.

The homestead became partially visible from a distance and Solomon didn't push the tired mule to go faster. It was hard to make much out and he was telling Sallie Mae more about his family and pointing out every trail and marker so excitedly that he didn't actually notice much. His wife was just looking everywhere absorbing her new home as much as possible.

As the house came into view, Sallie Mae's eyes were drawn far left toward the woods and she took Solomon's arm firmly. Her grip was so strong he pulled up the wagon and looked at her with questions in his eyes.

He slowly followed her sight line, noticing no movement around the homestead but nothing particularly out of order. Then he found the scene she saw and he gasped and took her hand in his so firmly that she feared her fingers would squeeze right off.

She wiggled her hand a little so he would loosen his grip. Without turning his head he said, "I'm sorry, Gal, didn't mean to hurt you." He murmured, "Don't look good," then took a deep breath and studied the group.

Sallie had already begun to count, based on all of his descriptions of the people most dear to him. "I can tell there's little Sarah and Richard."

Watching the people, their heads downward, who hadn't heard the wagon, Solomon went on. "Granny, Mama, . . . there's Pete and Betsy."

"Solomon? There's men I can't pick out . . ." She didn't want to say it.

"Papa . . . oh, no, Papa."

Sallie Mae had barely heard him but he confirmed what she felt and feared. She placed her hand flat on his back offering him calm. "Breathe in, husband." Husband -- the word still sounded foreign but in a wonderful, mystical way. "Breathe in and breathe out."

Fearful of disrupting the service yet wanting to embrace his mother and sister who must both be heartbroken, Solomon gripped the reins as though his life depended on them. The heads in the circle rose and figures began to slowly turn and move out and away from the circle. Still he was frozen.

"Slow," said his wife, her hand on his back right where his heart was, "go slow and give them time to shift to you."

The mule plodded toward the yard at the heart of the homestead and Solomon, his voice cracking, said, "Looks like we gonna be grown up for sure now."

Her left hand remained on his back reading his heart and her right reached for his wrist where her thumb rested on the point she knew she could feel his pulse. When her thumb made contact, he felt their joining in his heart and throughout his body – pulse to pulse. Solomon sat straight and strong. "Good Book says there's a time for everything. This is our time of testin' and we can do it long as we're together."

"You a man full, Mr. Solomon Freeman, and you'll know what to do and say when time comes long as we strong in the Lord." His new bride wanted to say and do the right things, too, and she knew how very important Solomon's father was to him. "You go on acting like your Papa watchin', and talk to him like he listenin', and he help you know the right ways." Her left hand made slow circles on his back and his racing heart calmed.

"Before I left to come to you he told me."

"He was proud of you, Solomon, and he knew he had a good son."

The wagon stopped at the edge of the yard. A slight smile came to his lips and he prayed, "Thank you, Jesus, he said it. Papa told me he loved me."

Historical Notes

Amendment 15, ratified in February of 1870, allowed that the "right to vote shall not be denied or abridged on the basis of race, color or previous condition of servitude." It superseded state laws prohibiting blacks from voting. There were places that didn't agree with Amendment 15 and attempted, sometimes successfully, to block black voters. The 1872 presidential election, in which Moses finally voted, reelected Ulysses S. Grant.

Banking, at the time Pete opened his bank in Madison, was a risky endeavor. Banks were either chartered, registered with the state and enjoying a level of risk protection or insurance, or private, offering banking services with personal and/or invested funds without government guarantee. History shows that there were no chartered banks in Florida until at least two years after Pete Harker opened his bank. He was a man of means but needed additional investors, so he went to Savannah and Charleston to meet with possible partners. Atlanta was so devastated during the Civil War the financial centers shifted to Savannah and Charleston, at least temporarily. We don't know by the end of *Man 'Most Grown* whether Pete's risk is successful or not; I like to think it was!

Canned Milk might have been a luxury for most people of the late nineteenth century. Fortunately, it was available when Lela needed it for Sarah. A good guess would be that they had evaporated milk because it is thinner and less processed but that isn't the first canned milk produced. What Lela would have had was condensed milk. It was highly processed and thick so the contents of one can provided more servings than a can of evaporated or the same measure of fresh milk. For more information contact: **www.bordendairy.com.**

Carpetbaggers were northerners who went south after the Civil War and suspected by Southerners of taking advantage of them through political or business dealings. A carpetbag was a common large hand-carried traveling satchel made of a carpet-like material, thus the name carpetbagger. These people traveled lightly moving from place to place quickly with their swindles and cons. The unethical practices of the few left bad tastes in the mouths of many southerners and the term became one of derision applied to any outsider who didn't fit in and wasn't trusted.

A *Cord of Wood* (4x8x2 ft.) is a common measure of chopped firewood. Wood was cut into two foot lengths and split into manageable diameter to fit into a typical fireplace. These two foot lengths were neatly arranged in a stack eight feet long and four feet high. The cords were often covered to keep the wood dry. Because firewood was essential for cooking, heat, meat curing, and laundering it was an almost constant chore priority.

Cow Hunting was the early pioneer practice of gathering small groups of unclaimed woods cows into a herd. Once a region was well settled, animals were branded annually and then allowed to free graze. After calving season, neighbors worked to round up all of the animals. Calves were branded to match their mothers and identify their owners, sale animals were taken to market, and the rest were released back into the wild. Like Cracker horses, these Cracker cattle were remnants of the earliest Spanish settlers who brought livestock to Florida. Their cousins, the Texas Longhorns, were also introduced by the Spanish. Cracker cows, however, evolved with shorter horns because of the thick growth of the area and smaller because of the less protein-rich grass in many areas they grazed.

Cracker Cures, also called folk remedies, refer to the traditional medical treatments passed through generations. Often doctors were not available and local women (often called Granny Doctors) or family members who demonstrated skill in healing did their best with what they knew and the materials they had. Generally, these practices were a blend of natural heading remedies and superstition. Some Cracker cures seem ridiculous, such as placing and ax under the bed to cut after pain from childbirth, tying a string around the ankles or wrists to keep off arthritis, and rubbing the head morning and evening with onions until is it red then rubbing it with honey to repair baldness. Others (many still used today) have proved to be practical, useful, and effective treatments. These include tobacco juice relieving the pain of bee stings, turpentine relieving pain and speeding healing on a wound, clumps of cobwebs stemming bleeding, and sassafras tea calming nerves and soothing sore throats. Nature provided herbs, plant parts, and soil types that were combined to make teas salves, and poultices. In fact, many modern day medicines, such as aspirin, have their origin from these very treatments from nature.

Dudley Farm, located four miles east of Newberry, Florida, in Alachua County, is an authentic operational nineteenth-century farmstead. During the time of Solomon's story, Civil War Captain P. B. H. Dudley, Sr. lived in a log cabin less than a mile north of the current farmstead, which was notbuilt until the 1880s. However, many of the farm's practices are little changed from Solomon's time. At Dudley Farm visitors see the original two-story home of P. B. H. Dudley, Jr. and his large family, with its surrounding kitchen, barns, and store -- unique because the structures are original, not reproductions. The farmstead is populated by heritage livestock and crops. For more information contact: Dudley Farm historic Sate Park, 18730 West Newberry Road, Newberry, Florida 32669, phone 352-472-1142.

Getzen, Thomas is the only real person in *Man 'Most Grown* other than Captain and Mrs. Dudley. Mr. Getzen lost a leg in the war and sold his farm in South Carolina, then moved to Ft. White where he built a large two story home for his growing family. College educated, Mr. Getzen was a successful farmer and would have been the kind of client Pete Harker would seek. The *Solomon* story web continues. One of Thomas Getzen's sons, Samuel Pace Getzen (named for Thomas's father) was a doctor in Newberry near Dudley Farm and Dr. Getzen's son, Samuel Pace Getzen, Jr. developed his lifelong love of horses as a boy at his grandfather Thomas' farm in Ft. White. Eventually, Robert J. (Bobby) Barry sought to identify Cracker Horse owners and with a committed partner in his brother-in-law, Sam Getzen, Jr. and others the Florida Cracker Horse Association was organized and is credited with saving the breed from extinction.

Marshtackies or *Cracker Horses*, like Cracker cattle, came to Florida when the Spanish claimed the state. The Spanish brought livestock and long, black, whips to control the beasts. The cracking sound of those skillfully used whips is the origin of the term "Cracker." Cracker horses (they are not ponies) are smaller and more slender than typical cow horses, but their strength and endurance are legendary. They are characterized by an extremely smooth gait and are still widely used by Florida cattlemen. Since 1989 the Florida Cracker Horse Association has registered qualified horses and preserved their heritage and lineage before their line was lost completely. For more information contact: The Florida Cracker Horse Association, 2992 Lake Bradford Rd. South, Tallahassee, FL 32310 **www.floridacrackerhorses.com**.

New Troy was the primary town in 1860s and 70s Lafayette County and served as county seat for several decades. By the time New Troy was destroyed by fire, the settlement (fictionally called Fayettetown in the book) grew up, was named Mayo, and became the county seat. New Troy was approximately six miles southeast of present-day Mayo.

Southern Homestead Act of 1862 and its broader implementation during Reconstruction provided for immigrants, former slaves, and displaced farmers to earn homesteads. Blacks could homestead 80 acres while whites could claim 160 acres. Building a dwelling, working the land for five years, and paying a $10 filing fee gave the homesteader his patent deed. Land could also be purchased for $1.25 an acre, but 80 acres would have cost $100, cash was rare, and $100 would have been a large sum in that day. Often the available land was unproductive, resulting in years of hard work and eventual failure. Former slaves were not encouraged to be or readily accepted as homesteaders. Although the Freemans struggled mightily, they benefitted from their favored status on Mr. Walker's plantation and had more tools and supplies than most in their position. Black or white, an entire family often worked and saved for years to accumulate even a minimum payment in cash.

Way Key is the location of the town of Cedar Key on the Gulf Coast of central Florida. The group of small islands are generally considered a unit and referred to as Cedar Key(s). The islands' history is a litany of small communities, rail and ship transport, and hurricane destruction. At the time Pete and Solomon were driving cattle there, the railroad trestle from the mainland south to Way Key had been rebuilt after Union Army damage during the Civil War. The actual town of Cedar Key was on the small island of Atsena Otie Key located directly south of Way Key and accessed by small boat. There was a modest port on Way Key from which seven steamer lines ran regular routes to Mobile, Alabama; New Orleans, Louisiana; and Galveston, Texas. It is also reasonable to think there would have been Cuban ships venturing as far north as Way Key for trade. Despite its return to commerce, Civil War damage was evident and neither Way Key nor Atsena Otie was alluring to visitors. A hurricane in 1896 destroyed everything on the smaller island and the town of Cedar Key moved from Atsena Otie to Way Key where it remains today.

Windshake is the term given to the slight crack in the center of a tree. When chopping firewood the two foot log is stood upright for splitting; depending upon its size it would be split into two or four smaller logs. The log is turned so the windshake is perpendicular to the chopper. This small split at the center of the log is caused by the prevailing winds blowing the tree as it grew and is what allows the tree to bend flexibly without snapping against the wind. If the axe hits the shake, the log splits much more easily.

Bibliography

The following resources were consulted while researching *Man 'Most Grown.*

Books

Clark, James C. *100 Quick Looks at Florida History*. Sarasota, Florida: Pineapple Press. 2000.

Dovell, J. E. *The History of Banking in Florida: 1828-1954*. Gannon, Michael. The New History of Florida. Gainesville, Florida: University Press of Florida. 1996.

Morris, Allen. *Florida Place Names*. Sarasota, Florida: Pineapple Press. 1995.

Pickard, Ben. *Dudley Farm: A History of Florida Farm Life*. Gainesville, Florida: Alachua Press, Inc. 2003.

Wood, Cedric Stephen. *Cracker Cures*. Arcadia, Florida: Peace River Valley Historical Society. 1978.

Articles and Booklets

"A History of Cedar Key," *Cedar Key Beacon* (February, 1990).

Bailey, Nelson. "Florida's 'Little' Horses: A Little Amble Through Florida History." *Horse & Pony* (January 5, 1993).

Getzen, Samuel P. "Cracker Horses." The Florida Cracker Horse Association, Inc. Newberry, Florida (1992).

Websites

Florida State Archives. *Jefferson County, Florida Freedmens' Contract, 1867* [online], [cited September 2002]. **(www.floridamemory.com)**

National Park Service. *Homestead Act of 1862*. [online]. Washington, D. C.: [cited August 2005]. **(www.nps.gov)**

Other

Dudley Farm Historic State Park Archives.
　　Newberry, Florida, 2004
Getzen, Samuel P. "Getzen Family History." Interviews.
　　2010.

Acknowledgements

This book has been a long time coming. It is harder to write a sequel because everything must correlate with the first, must make sense to those who haven't read the first, and must be new and different for those who have. But, at the insistence of more than I can count, I realized that more of Solomon's story needed to be told. For many reasons this was a tough one to finish. I'm forever grateful to all of those at church, the post office, grocery store, and most everywhere else who asked when there would be more of Solomon's story. I hope this gives you all satisfaction that his story turns out pretty well after all and that he'll be just fine.

I knew Solomon would need to face some man-sized challenges, but as the story unfolded it was hard to put him through such struggles and particularly hard to end the way it did. I could finally make the hard decisions and write the final chapter when my own beloved father, Marion Bishop, died at 95. I'm thankful our relationship was closer than Solomon's and Moses' and we were blessed to have him in our lives so long. He was instrumental in *Solomon's* agricultural accuracy and was a voracious reader. We enjoyed many hours of reading together in his last years. He remained incredibly sharp and had heard – **and vetted** – about two-thirds of *Man 'Most Grown* before God called him home. When I sat to write, that tiny final chapter came to me with such clarity, I suppose I had to live it before I could write it for Solomon.

My husband, Bob, has been so supportive as I reach points when I pour time into a writing project and I appreciate his patience. It can't be easy dealing with that kind of erratic creativity. My long time pals, The Beach Buddies and The Grant Girls are always in my corner and ready to be sounding boards, advisors, proofreaders, and cheerleaders. As with *Solomon*, Nancy Galloway gave Manuel his Spanish voice and Dr. Ana Shaw advised on medical issues. Our sister-in-law, Annette Toy Shaw created the cover art and Jason Taylor turned that into the cover.

My hope is that you've enjoyed the story and, in doing so, you've learned a little and better appreciated some of the lesser-known heritage of our varied and fascinating state.

As always, happy reading,

Marilyn

If you read this before reading *Solomon*, do go back and read all of the adventures that got the Freemans where you met them. Also, check out *In Another Time,* also historical but this time with romance and mystery. All are available in print and ebooks on Amazon. Signed books may be ordered from my website (relaunched by early summer) at **www.marilynbishopshaw.com**. I'd love to hear from you at mbshawwrite.aol.com.

Made in the USA
Charleston, SC
04 January 2017